NOBODY'S ROGUE

ROGUES OF REDEMPTION, BOOK 4

BY
BRENNA ASH

Dragonblade Publishing, Inc. is an imprint of Kathryn Le Veque Novels, Inc.
P.O. Box 23
Moreno Valley, CA 92556
ceo@dragonbladepublishing.com

Produced in the United States of America

First Edition December 2024
Print Edition

ARE YOU SIGNED UP FOR DRAGONBLADE'S BLOG?

You'll get the latest news and information on exclusive giveaways, exclusive excerpts, coming releases, sales, free books, cover reveals and more.

Check out our complete list of authors, too!

No spam, no junk. That's a promise!

Sign Up Here

www.dragonbladepublishing.com

Dearest Reader;

Thank you for your support of a small press. At Dragonblade Publishing, we strive to bring you the highest quality Historical Romance from some of the best authors in the business. Without your support, there is no 'us', so we sincerely hope you adore these stories and find some new favorite authors along the way.

Happy Reading!

CEO, Dragonblade Publishing

Additional Dragonblade books by Author Brenna Ash

Rogues of Redemption Series
Sweet Rogue O' Mine (Book 1)
Rogue You Like a Hurricane (Book 2)
No Rogue Like You (Book 3)
Nobody's Rogue (Book 4)

CHAPTER ONE

May 1813
Northern Spain

HIDDEN DEEP IN the shadows within the copse of trees, Malcolm Kennedy leaned against a sturdy pine, his eyes focused on the dark figure sneaking through the wet grass, dangerously close to crossing over enemy lines.

Wellington, the general leading their troops, had tasked him with uncovering the traitor—a mission he'd happily accepted. In the days since, Malcolm had been waiting patiently for the man to make his move.

He much preferred his work away from the front lines. Not that he wouldn't fight if needed, he most certainly would. But discovering enemy secrets and rooting out traitors was something he excelled at.

Observation was his strongest skill, and he'd made quite the name for himself because of it. So much so, that Wellington had personally sought him out and confided in him that there was a mole amongst their ranks.

Someone was leaking their plans to the French, and they needed to be stopped.

Now.

As he continued to study the mysterious figure, he narrowed his eyes.

The suspect's shoulders were hunched, his gait lacked confidence and finesse, leading Malcolm to believe the person he trailed was of lower ranking. A foot soldier mayhap.

The sound of the leaves crunching beneath the figure's footsteps halted. Unfortunately, no matter how hard he tried, the inky darkness made it impossible for Malcolm to discern any distinguishing features, leaving him unable to identify the suspect.

Malcolm moved forward, his breathing low, boots silent on the soft ground. Stealth was another skill he possessed.

His pulse quickened as he drew closer, the rush of the chase breathing new life into his war-weary bones.

Almost daily, he missed Scotland, his home country, and Culzean Castle, his familial estate. He would be happy to be back on familiar land. After being away for far too long he had begun to worry if he would ever return to his beloved home.

The interloper tripped over a rock and crashed to the ground on to his hands and knees.

"Oof." He scrambled back to his feet and brushed his hands off on his thighs.

Malcolm stepped from behind the tree, approached the figure, and stopped a short distance from his back. He clamped a heavy hand down on top of the man's shoulder and spun him around.

A most unmanly *squeal* escaped the man's, nay, the lad's lips. After a moment of shock, he twisted and jerked, breaking free, then took off running toward the enemy and their makeshift barracks just over the knoll.

"Shite," Malcolm cursed and sprinted after the boy. He abhorred running, but there was no other option but to give chase.

It was critical he captured him before he crested the hill.

The culprit held his cap to his head as he dashed through the brush.

He was fast, but Malcolm was faster. Once he was within a few feet of his target, he put his head down and lunged, tackling the boy to the ground.

The boy's cap flew off and his mouth gaped open and closed as he struggled to take in a breath. Like a fish after being pulled from a river. He threw his arms up to his head in an effort to defend himself from possible blows.

"Let...me...go." He sucked in air between each word, desperately trying to catch his stolen breath.

"Be still." Malcolm held him face down on the ground with one knee pressed to the center of his back. He patted him down, dug through the boy's pockets, pulled off his boots, searching for evidence he was their traitor.

His fingers closed around a roll of papers secured to the boy's back by a leather strap around his waist.

A slow smile crept across Malcolm's face.

"Well, well," he whispered, as he yanked it free. "What have we here?"

"Give those back..." The lad struggled against Malcolm's hold in a feeble attempt to snatch the papers away.

"Now, now." Malcolm pressed his knee harder into the lad's back. "We shall have none of that."

He unrolled the documents, and a brief glance confirme d they were the ones he sought.

Confident he had captured their traitor, he rolled up the papers and tucked them away in his own inner coat pocket. He flipped the lad to his back, grabbed a handful of the front of his shirt, and lifted him until he balanced on the tips of his toes. Malcolm shifted until the moonlight shined on the turncoat's face, and he got his first look at their traitor.

"Angus?" Betrayal tingled across Malcolm's skin like the sting of embers from a fire. Angus worked for him.

The lad hung his head briefly, then lifted it to look toward the top of the knoll separating him from his supposed salvation.

"Ye will find no help there." He gave him a quick shake to regain his attention. "What the hell were ye thinking, lad?"

"I was thinking that this war needs to come to an end." His tone was defiant as he spat out the words.

"By giving our information to the enemy?" Malcolm pinched the bridge of his nose and shook his head in disbelief. "But, why? Why would ye do such a thing?"

"Too many have died."

"Your treachery has contributed to that.

Angus threw his shoulders back in a sudden burst of confidence.

"Ye havena any idea of what 'tis like to no' have e'erything ye need," he sneered. "To want naught but to see your family thrive."

"Ye traded our secrets for coin?" Malcolm could not keep the disgust and disappointment from his voice.

The lad refused to look him in the eye.

Angus had always seemed eager to help. Eager to please, and to get them whatever they needed. Now Malcolm understood why. Because the more he could put himself into the areas of conversation, the more information he could garner to sell out his country.

Of all the people they had working with them, Angus was the very last person he would have thought would betray their country. Malcolm had taken the lad under his wing and had vowed to himself to ensure Angus returned to his family, alive and well, after the war.

"Did ye really think this would end the war?" He patted the chest of his coat, above where the documents were concealed. "And if so, what of your family that ye are doing this for? If we dinna win the war, what do ye think will come of your family then?" He sighed and shook his head. "Give me your wrists, Angus."

After securing him with the leather strap he'd used for the documents, Malcolm wrapped his long fingers around the boy's upper arm. As he led them back to their encampment, he was filled with dread at the fate awaiting young Angus.

His actions were indefensible. And even if Malcolm did speak up on his behalf—which he would not—naught would change. The treachery was too deep and too much information had been sold, putting them at a dangerous disadvantage against Napoleon's forces and costing lives. Lives of people Malcolm had considered friends.

Two days later, he watched as Angus was hanged from a noose for his crimes.

Malcolm's job was done. He had accomplished the task he'd been given. But his heart was heavy with regret for the life Angus would never have, and his soul was blackened by a betrayal he would not soon forget.

CHAPTER TWO

August 1816
Twynholm, Scotland

"AH, MY LORD." Viscount Wilson extended his arm and greeted Malcolm with a handshake and a quick bow of his head as he entered the library. "I thank ye for agreeing to attend and monitor our guests. With the thief still roaming the countryside, I immediately thought of ye to ensure our valuables stay within our own walls. My wife is verra concerned."

A stealthy thief had been taking advantage of estate owners while they were preoccupied with the hustle and bustle of hosting balls and parties to steal from the owners undetected. Viscount Wilson, like many of the other nobles, was rightfully concerned he and his wife would be the next victims.

"Of course, my lord." Malcolm looked forward to the distraction. He missed the excitement of the chase. The secrecy of the mission.

As the Earl of Cassilis, running the day-to-day operations of Culzean Castle and its surrounding lands, as well as his additional holdings, occupied his time. But he was bored with the monotony of signing papers and poring over books and accounts. He was lucky that when he returned from the war, his estate had been handled properly.

He knew many that hadn't had such an easy return home, his best friends included.

So, while he was grateful, he grew tired of the doldrum.

Malcolm needed action to fill his days.

When he received the letter from the viscount about his upcoming ball in Twynholm, he'd nearly tossed the invitation in the fire—until his eyes fell upon the first line.

I need your expertise...

Intrigued, Malcolm read on to learn of Wilson's worry that the thief, who had been dubbed the Phantom Prowler, would try to help himself to some of the many items of value held within Wilson's estate.

The absurd moniker came from the mystery surrounding the thief's true identity. Many believed he was someone in high society, since nearly every ball or party host had fallen victim. But just as easily, it could be one of the victim's servants. There just wasn't enough information yet.

"Let me show ye the portion of the estate we would like to keep private, and, most importantly, free of guests or possible intruders." Wilson led the way.

Malcolm followed him out of the library and up the blue-carpeted stairs. From there, they walked down the hallway that led them to what Malcolm assumed was the viscount and viscountesses bed chambers.

"We may have guests up on this floor for various reasons, but our bed chambers are strictly off limits to everyone."

"That is understandable." Malcolm wouldn't want a stranger rummaging about in his bed chamber either.

The ornate door groaned as Wilson pushed it open, and Malcolm trailed him into what was clearly Lady Wilson's chamber.

He adjusted his cravat, uncomfortable in such a private space that should not be privy to his or any other man's eyes.

A canopied bed decorated in light-blue linens and piled high with lace-trimmed cream pillows was centered in the room. A white vanity table and large looking glass were set in one corner. A rolling tray filled with various bottles, jars, and tins of powders, lotions, and pomades, stood at the side of the table.

Against the far wall stood a large mahogany wardrobe. The viscount approached it, throwing the doors open wide.

"This, this is what I want ye to ensure stays intact." He pointed to a jewelry armoire tucked inside. "My wife covets her collection of jewels, and she would be devastated if even a single piece came up missing."

Malcolm straightened.

"I promise ye have naught to fash about, my lord." His confidence imbued in each word. "Lady Wilson's jewels will remain in her possession."

A smile spread across Wilson's ruddy face as he clapped his hands and rubbed them together with delight.

"I knew ye were the right man for the job, Lord Kennedy. Thanks to the fine work ye did with Wellington, your reputation is known throughout both the lowlands and the highlands." He clasped Malcom's shoulder as he led them out into the hall. "Uncovering that traitor who dared to sell us out to the enemy was quite the triumph." He clapped him on the shoulder and dropped his hand. "Excellent work."

Malcolm forced a tight smile, because the memories still burned.

Angus had been old enough to know of his wrongdoing. But seven and ten was too young to have one's life snuffed out. There was much he could have accomplished, had he only chosen a different path.

He cleared his throat to rid his mind of his morbid thoughts and focused on the task at hand.

"What time do ye expect your guests to begin arriving?" He followed the viscount down the stairs.

Happy for the distraction of discussions surrounding the event, Malcolm listened as Wilson babbled on about who he expected to be in attendance at this evening's ball.

"We've invited Gunn Burnett, Laird of Leys, as well," Wilson said.

It made sense, after all, Twynholm was close to Gunn's southern estate. It had been some time since they'd seen each other, and since they were the only two unmarried men left in their group of friends, it was important they stick together. Malcolm's spirits lifted upon hearing that one of his best friends might make an appearance.

⫸⫸⫷⫷

ANNABEL "LIZZIE" BARCLAY fussed with the front of her gown.

"Ye have your invitation, Miss?" Mary, her maid and someone she considered a friend, had been going on incessantly and ensuring she did not forget her party invitation.

"Aye, Mary." Lizzie rolled her eyes and sighed loudly. "'Tis the tenth time ye've asked me such."

"I am only making certain that ye can attend the party, Miss." Her maid could be quite fretful at times.

"Look," Lizzie reached into her reticule and pulled out the rectangle paper, waving it in the air. "See? 'Tis right here." It was actually her parents' invitation had they decided to attend—which they did not, due to prior engagements.

"Will ye approach Lady Wilson?" Mary's brown brows furrowed in concern.

Lizzie turned in her chair and grasped her maid's hands.

"Dinna fash, Mary. I only intend to recover my dear grandmama's jewelry. She kept her tone light, unconcerned. "Once I have it back in my possession, I will exit the party promptly."

"I still dinna think much of your plan, Miss." Mary worried her bottom lip. "What if ye are caught?"

"I shan't be." Lizzie gave her hands a gentle squeeze, released them, and stood. She strolled over to the large window and gazed out into the dusky evening. "I will be verra careful." She looked over her shoulder and smiled at her maid. "I promise."

"If your parents were to find out what ye are truly doing..." she whispered and continued wringing her hands together, leaving the unspoken words hanging in the air like a heavy cloud on the rainiest of days.

"Mary, cease these negative thoughts at once." She whisked them away with a flick of her wrist. "They will no' find out, and ye will no' tell them either."

"'Tis my duty to keep ye safe, Miss. We already are no' where we said we would be."

That was true. She had convinced her parents to let her travel south to visit a close friend that had recently moved to Twynholm. Once she had seen the invitation her parents had received requesting their presence at the Wilsons' ball, she knew it was her chance.

Intrigued by the Phantom Prowler, she'd followed the articles published in the papers with a great deal of enthusiasm. However, when jewels had disappeared from her own home, Tolton Hall, her countenance went from titillation to anger.

Gone were her grandmama's jewelry. A beautiful pair of earrings bedecked with stunning sapphires of the deepest blue, and a necklace to match. Lizzie had always loved staring at them in her mother's jewelry armoire. They reminded her of her beloved grandmama and the close relationship they'd shared. When she passed two years ago, Lizzie was bereft. She missed her dearly and thought of her every day.

With the precious pieces gone, she'd set about to uncover the prowler and recover the jewels that were rightfully hers. Now she was certain she'd figured out the identity of the Phantom Prowler.

Unlike the papers who thought the thief was a man, Lizzie kenned better. Nay, the thief was a woman. A viscountess no less.

Lizzie cared naught if Viscountess Wilson continued with her thievery. The woman's secret was safe with her. All she wanted was her grandmama's jewels back.

She was determined that, before the night was over, she would have regained possession of what rightfully belonged to her.

In the morn, with jewels in her hand, she and Mary would leave and return to Stonehaven and Tolton Hall.

No one would have been harmed, and no one would be the wiser. She believed her plan was foolproof.

"I dinna care for it, Miss."

Realizing she would not sway Lizzie to change her mind, Mary finally shook her head. "But ye will do as ye wish either way."

"All will be well, Mary." She dropped back onto the chair and studied her reflection in the looking glass. "Blast this hair." She huffed out a breath, and the dark curl that had fallen on her forehead fluttered. It was a constant battle to keep that one curl under control. She swore its life's purpose was to annoy her to the ends of the earth.

"Ye have lovely locks." Mary approached and picked up the brush from the vanity and began pulling it through Lizzie's thick waves. "Have ye a particular style in mind for your hair tonight?"

Lizzie thought about it for a moment and came to the conclusion that she didn't. "Nay, Mary. Ye have free rein to do what ye will." A huge grin broke out on Lizzie's face. "Surprise me."

Almost three hours later, Lizzie smiled at the Wilson's butler.

"Good evening." She greeted and handed him her parents' invitation, and holding her breath for fear she'd be turned away.

"Welcome, Miss Barclay." The elderly man bowed, and, with a sweep of his slender arm, allowed her entry.

She breathed a sigh of relief when his attention was immediately drawn to the next person arriving.

Well, that was simple.

Lizzie made her way to the ballroom, carefully surveying the halls as she passed. One of those corridors would lead her to the treasure she sought. But which one? She would have to pay attention and gauge the best time for her to slip away and start her exploration.

Her heart jumped in her chest so forcefully, she was certain any-one standing nearby would hear it over the orchestra playing on the stage.

The ballroom was decorated in an autumnal theme. Flowers of orange, brown, and gold arranged in huge vases were positioned in the center of each round table in the room. The table coverings were the color of tree bark, adding to the overall nature feel of the party.

Fallen leaves had been collected and used to make garland that hung in various places throughout the room.

Eliminate the music and the light din of conversation, and it was like walking through the woods on a late September evening.

"Viscountess Wilson." Lizzie greeted the hostess with a curtsy. "Your estate is lovely. The decorations are absolutely stunning and fitting for the time of year."

"Thank ye." The woman gave her a polite society smile, cocked her head, and studied her.

Lizzie realized the viscountess had no idea who she was. Which made sense—it had been years since they had seen each other, back when Lizzie was a young lass.

"I apologize, my lady. Lizzie Barclay. My parents send their apolo-gies."

"Ah, aye." Her smile warmed. "I was sorry to hear your parents were unable to attend. 'Tis sweet of ye to appear in their absence."

"I happened to be in the area visiting a dear friend and thought it was only right since ye and the viscount were so kind to extend the invitation." *And it gives me the opportunity to retrieve what belongs to me.*

"I do hope ye enjoy your evening," the viscountess said.

"Thank ye." She curtsied and her hostess moved away.

As Lizzie watched her smile and greet her other guests in her magnificent gown and perfectly coiffed hair, she never would have suspected the viscountess was the Phantom Prowler. It was only with her dogged determination that she was able to uncover the viscountess as the thief. She pored over articles published in the papers, taking note of all the details of the robberies. She paid attention to those who were in attendance at the balls, until all was revealed. It could be no one else but her.

Considering the opulence on full display in the estate, lack of money did not seem to be of worry. Of course, it could all be a facade but, if it were, it was extremely elaborate and quite convincing.

Nay, she was certain the Wilsons were quite wealthy.

Lizzie accepted an offered flute of champagne from a passing servant. The fizzy bubbles tickled her nose as she took a small sip. As much as she would love naught more than to down the entire glass for the courage it would offer, she needed to keep all her senses in check. It was the only way to ensure her plan would be successful.

Fiddling with the dance card tied around her wrist, she tried to hide it inside her glove. She was not interested in attracting the attention of anyone of the opposite sex this night. The more people who took notice of her, the harder it would be for her to slip away. For that very reason, she looked around and slunk toward the edges of the room. She stood near the tall double doors decorated with white trim that led to the living quarters and surely the master chambers of both the viscount and viscountess.

Everything she knew about women of her hostess's standing told Lizzie she would find her grandmama's jewelry stowed somewhere in the viscountess's chamber. That was where she needed to begin her search.

Movement from the other side of the door caught her attention. She turned and her breath hitched when her gaze clashed with stormy blue eyes belonging to one of the most handsome faces she had ever had the pleasure of seeing.

Just as quickly as the connection was made, it was lost when he turned and walked in the opposite direction. As he spoke with the viscount, she examined the way his broad shoulders stretched the seams of his coat. Lizzie hadn't the faintest idea who the man was, but her curiosity was piqued, and should he approach her and ask her to dance, she would not deny him.

So much for swearing off dancing for the night.

"Concentrate, Lizzie," she mumbled to herself.

She gave a quick shake of her head to rid her mind of thoughts of the mystery man, sipped her champagne, and against her better judgement, went ahead and finished the entire glass.

A warm feeling enveloped her, which she attributed to the champagne working its way through her body, and not the handsome stranger whose brief glance still lingered on her skin.

CHAPTER THREE

MALCOLM STOOD IN the corner of the ballroom, nursing a glass of much-too-sweet punch. It was a taste he found most unpleasant. The drink should be reserved for children, not given to grown adults trying to escape the boredom of what their life had become. What he really wanted was a dram of whisky. Mayhap two.

He scanned the attendees and was almost certain that the coin the viscount had paid Malcolm for his "security expertise" was a wasted investment.

The ball was a drab affair, but he was thankful to be staying on the outskirts of the party and not be the focus of the mamas pushing their daughters of marrying age upon every eligible man in the room. Being unavailable to sign the lasses' dance cards was a welcome happenstance. The men being ambushed on the floor looked flustered at the best and miserable at worst.

His mission to remain undetected from the focused search of the women had so far been successful.

No one in attendance had caught his curiosity. Most were too loud and wanting to be the center of attention to be capable of slinking about unnoticed to pilfer the host's jewels.

Then he saw the raven-haired lass with wide brown eyes and he suddenly had a person of interest. But not because she looked suspicious. Nay, not at all. When their eyes collided, a jolt of heat surged through him before he quickly looked away. It had been too long since he'd lost himself in the soft curves of a lass. His body's sudden reaction was an unfriendly reminder of just exactly how long it had been.

A bonnie lass was not the reason he was here, though. Even if he doubted that the Phantom Prowler would make an appearance, making Malcolm's presence unnecessary, it didn't mean that he could turn his attentions elsewhere. His work ethic would not allow it.

Unable to ignore the pull, he slid his gaze over to the lass once again. Her full bosom tested the bodice of her rose-colored gown. White gloves covered her hands to her slim, upper arms. Her fair skin reminded him of the finest porcelain. Her soft curves beckoned him.

He cleared his throat, dragging his stare away from her and cursed his wandering thoughts as they began to wonder what was hidden behind the silky material she wore.

Before temptation overcame him and he found himself once again focusing on the lass, he turned in the opposite direction and moved to the other side of the room, putting distance between them.

Standing in a corner, he squared his shoulders, and turned to the crowd gathered on the dance floor, the heels of the dancing couples' shoes creating a steady staccato that echoed throughout the room. A servant carrying a tray of champagne passed and Malcolm reached out, trading his punch for something slightly more palatable.

At least he knew the champagne wouldn't dull his senses.

A strong hand clapped him on the shoulder, causing him to jolt and the champagne to splash on his hand. He turned to see Gunn smiling broadly.

The spilled champagne forgotten, he grinned. "Brother," Malcolm greeted his close friend, and they shook hands enthusiastically, clapping each other on the back. "'Tis been too long since I've last seen ye."

Gunn nodded, his brow furrowing. "Aye. Business has kept me close to home."

"All is well, I hope?"

Gunn's eyes darkened, his smile faltering for a moment before he replaced it with a grin. "Ne'er better."

Malcolm kenned his friend lied. But if Gunn wanted him to ken all the details, he would have disclosed them, so he didn't push. Instead, he quickly changed the subject.

"Are ye ready to be bombarded by all the mamas? They seem to be particularly honed in on eligible bachelors this eve."

Just as Gunn opened his mouth to answer, the shrill call of one of the aforementioned mamas rang out, piercing the air. Malcolm blanched at the most uncomely sound and discreetly backed away, ignoring Gunn's silent plea for help.

"My lord," a woman called to Gunn, pushing her daughter toward him. "I would like to introduce ye to my daughter…"

Malcolm didn't stay within earshot any longer, instead opting to walk around the outer perimeter of the ballroom once again. His eyes studied every male in attendance, but didn't notice anyone acting out of sorts or suspicious in any way.

He scanned the room, looking for the raven-haired lass to no avail. Mayhap she also deemed the party a bore and took an early leave. He'd be lying if he said he was surprised. Deciding there was naught in the ballroom to see, he slipped out into the corridor. The air in the hall was slightly cooler and the area much quieter. He took a deep breath and enjoyed a brief respite.

Walking the length of the hall, he checked to ensure doors to rooms that were off-limits remained shut. As expected, everything was as it should be.

He passed the stairway that led to the upper rooms and the viscount and viscountess's chambers. That was when he heard it. The slightest creak of a door upstairs.

So quiet, if he hadn't been paying careful attention he would have missed it. Looking back toward the ballroom doors, he noted the hall was empty.

Mayhap he was wrong about the prowler. Mayhap the fool *was* daft enough to attempt a theft kenning that Malcolm was here to prevent that very thing.

He slipped up the stairs, careful to not make any noise as he kept to the carpeted center. On the second floor, he paused, ears straining for any additional noise.

Another creak and his head snapped to the area of the sound. The viscountess's chamber. He knew for a fact the viscountess was downstairs playing hostess alongside her husband. She would not be in her bedchamber.

But someone was.

Creeping down the hall, he stayed close to the wall. As he neared the room, he could hear rustling of things being moved about as if someone was rifling through something.

He paused outside the door and waited. The rustling continued so whoever was inside didn't hear his approach.

It appeared the viscount's investment was well-spent this eve after all. The door was slightly ajar, but the dark room didn't allow him to deduce who was inside—other than it was someone who shouldn't be there.

Carefully, he nudged the door slightly wider so he could slip through, thankful that the hinges were well-oiled and remained silent, not alerting the thief to his presence. His pistol was strapped into a holster hidden under his jacket.

Pulling it out, he pointed it at the figure hunched over the viscountess's jewelry chest and cocked the hammer. "I suggest ye back away from the jewels," he said quietly, his voice a dire warning.

The figure jumped back with a yelp, and clenched a handful of jewels to...

...her chest.

Hell's teeth. It was the lass from earlier.

"Please," she whispered, her hands up in defense. "Ye dinna understand."

He holstered his pistol. He wasn't going to shoot the lass.

This was an interesting turn of events. He'd never expected the prowler to be a lass. No one did. All the papers spoke of the thief being a man. And she was most definitely no man.

"These are mine." She dangled what appeared to be a necklace in front of her. "Well, no' mine, exactly," she stammered.

"Exactly, indeed. They belong to the viscountess." He shook his head with an unbelievable laugh and wagged a finger at the lass. "Ye are good. I will give ye that. Ye had all of us fooled thinking ye were a man."

Moonlight filtered in through the window and he could see her expression change from despair to dawning.

"I am no thief."

"Those items in your hand say otherwise."

"These are mine." She raised her fist to him, which he found comical, but he hid his laughter. She was a thief after all.

"Just a moment ago, ye said they werena yours." He crossed his arms. "What say ye to that?"

"They belong to my grandmother." A frown creased her forehead. "Belonged. She has passed on."

His heart tugged in his chest, and he tamped the unexpected feeling down. This was no time for sentiments. The lass was a thief. Though with how much noise she made, he hadn't the faintest idea how she hadn't been caught before now.

"I will call for the viscount. 'Tis up to him to decide what he would like to do with ye."

The lass rushed forward and grasped his sleeve.

"Nay, please dinna do that. I speak the truth. Do I look like a thief to ye?"

She did not, but he wasn't going to confess that to her.

"I can prove it to ye," she blurted out, nodding her head. "Aye.

There is a portrait in my family's home of my grandmother wearing these very pieces."

He lifted a brow at the lass as he studied her. Her stance seemed to lend truth to her statement, though she could just be a prolific deceiver along with being a prolific thief.

"It has taken me months to track these down. I wasna e'en certain they would be here until I actually found them."

What were the chances of there being two thief's stealing from party hosts? Nil, he concluded.

"The viscount could have your hand for such an offense. And that is no' taking into consideration any of the other burglaries ye have committed."

"I did no such thing!" she exclaimed, her voice a loud whisper. "Fine, ye want to call me a thief? Fine. But the only thing I have done is retrieve what is rightfully mine after having it stolen from me in the first place."

"Why would your supposedly stolen jewels be here?"

She shifted nervously, rolling her lips inward, clearly uncomfortable with the question.

"I willna answer that question," she said, stubbornly jutting her chin up to him. "Please, let me prove what I am saying to ye," she pleaded.

Something in her voice had him questioning his accusation of her. But he couldn't deny what he had seen with his own eyes.

But yet, she had his curiosity piqued. "Just how do ye expect to do that?"

"Follow me to Tolton Hall. I can prove it to ye there."

His brows lifted in surprise. If she truly were the prowler would she put forward such a request?

Aye, if she was conniving enough.

He couldn't help himself. "I'm unfamiliar with that residence. Where is it?"

"Stonehaven."

THE MAN LIZZIE had seen earlier stared at her as his jaw dropped. She had to make him believe her. The direness of her situation was not lost on her. He truly could turn her in to the viscount, who would have her prosecuted no doubt.

There would be no question of her guilt. He quite literally caught her with her hands in the viscountess's chest of jewels. Her family would be ruined.

She was thinking that she was starting to win him over, but then his gaze hardened and she wasn't so sure.

"Ye canna hand me over to the viscount," she pleaded as she clenched her fists, her grandmother's jewelry encased tightly in her fingers. She had searched far and wide. Diligently paid attention to who the thief could be.

She supposed she should be flattered the man standing before her thought her capable of pulling off such heists. But, really, now that she finally had what she'd came for, she just wanted to go back home.

"Ye are from Stonehaven?" His voice was quiet. Deep.

"Aye. I live there with my parents."

"Are they in attendance?"

She shook her head. Nay. All the more reason to wish that he didn't bring her to the viscount.

"Why no'?"

She threw her hands up in frustration. They needed to get out of this room. But instead, he wanted to engage in small talk. "They had other plans when the invitation arrived."

His eyes narrowed. "Do they ken ye are here?"

Worrying her lip with her teeth, she contemplated on whether or not she should tell him the truth. In the short time she'd spoken to him, she got the sense that the truth meant a lot to him. It did to her as well, but these circumstances were out of the norm.

He sighed and pushed a hand through his honey-colored hair. "Your hesitation to answer says more than your words e'er could."

"Please, sir. I promise ye, I am being truthful about the jewels. Truly, look in the chest. There are far more items of value there for the taking. If I was the thief dinna ye think I would take one of those or several of them? But I didna. Why? Because I got what I came for. I really can prove they belong to my family."

The man shook his head and snorted. "What's your name, Miss?"

"Lizzie," she answered without hesitation. She needed to earn his trust. She thought of Mary waiting outside. She would be most upset at the predicament she currently found herself in.

"Surname?"

"Barclay," she huffed. "And yours?" What's good for the goose is good for the gander. If she had to tell him who she was, he should have to do the same.

"Malcolm Kennedy, Earl of Cassilis."

Her eyes rounded. Of course he would be titled. She immediately dropped into a curtsy. "My lord."

He cocked his head to the side as he looked at her, and her skin heated from his scrutiny. The rays of the moonlight filtering in through the large windows, highlighted the planes of his face. His strong jaw and deep-set eyes. He was most handsome, and if circumstances were different, she might find herself trying to gain the earl's attention.

But right now she had his attention for all the wrong reasons.

He held his hand out, and she looked at it questioningly.

"The jewelry," he prompted, wiggling his fingers.

"'Tis mine," she stated stubbornly.

"So ye've said." He looked toward the door. "It willna be long afore my absence is noticed. If we are caught in here, both of us will pay the price."

"Ye believe me?" she asked hope blooming in her stomach.

"I am no' yet ready to say. However, I willna bring ye to the viscount's attention. But I will hold the pieces until I can be sure ye speak the truth."

She was grateful that he wasn't dragging her to the viscount and announcing to all that he'd caught the thief. But she didn't want to let go of her grandmother's jewelry. She'd worked so hard to track it down.

"This is what we will do. You will exit this room and ensure the staircase is clear before descending and then will wait in the foyer for me. I need to speak to the viscount."

"Nay!"

He stopped her with his hand in the air. "I will speak to the viscount to tell him that he has no worries this night and I will take my leave. The party will be ending shortly so it willna seem odd."

She waited for him to continue. All things considering, he was being much more kind than he needed to be.

"Fix the jewel chest so 'tis in the same condition ye found it," he ordered.

She scrambled to do just that. When she finished and he held out his hand, she sighed in defeat and dropped the jewelry in his large palm.

He pocketed the pieces and moved to the door, looking outside and then motioned for her to step forward.

"Remember, wait in the foyer. I will be there as soon as I can."

She nodded and stepped out of the room. His holding her jewelry ensured that she would be waiting for him whenever he returned. She couldn't very well leave without it. Not after coming all this way.

Descending the stairs quickly, she breathed a sigh of relief when the entryway was empty.

This night had not gone at all as she planned. She watched the earl come down the stairs and enter the ballroom, not sparing her a glance. She rolled her eyes. The earl was most businesslike.

He stopped to talk to a man, but it wasn't the viscount. They spoke in hushed tones, as if in serious conversation. Was he telling the man he'd caught the Phantom Prowler? Was he going to send him out to drag her to the authorities?

Her heart raced as she wrung her hands together and paced the floor. She was in trouble. Mary had been right. Why, oh why hadn't she listened to her maid? But Mary was more than that, she was also her friend.

The man the earl was talking to looked out the doors and glanced her way. Bile rose in her throat. The man was big and burly. He looked like he could be a boxer. Was he a jailer? Was he going to come and take her away?

Her breath quickened and she tried to ease them as she began to see black specks dance in her vision. It was suddenly so very hot. Between the heat and her racing heart, she could no longer keep herself standing.

And when the black specks became her whole vision and her world spun, her last thoughts were that she was a failure.

CHAPTER FOUR

MALCOLM PINCHED THE bridge of his nose and wondered what the hell he had just gotten himself into. He was talking to the viscount when a commotion in the corridor had caught their attention. They rushed out only to find Lizzie being helped up to her feet.

From what he'd been told, she'd fainted.

With an explanation of chivalry, he'd told the viscount that he would escort the lass home to ensure her safety.

Happy with that, the viscount bid him goodnight and returned to the ballroom.

Bother, that's what the lass was. Again, what had he gotten himself into?

Now, he waited outside the inn she and her maid were staying in whilst they visited Twynholm as they packed their things so they could begin their journey to Stonehaven. He had allowed them to sleep at the inn once he'd seen them back after the party. It made no sense to begin their travels at night. The roads were far too dangerous. He would have enough difficulty trying to get them to their destination in the light of day. There was no reason to make even more trouble for himself.

He supposed all wasn't lost. He'd been looking for excitement and he had found it.

Pulling his pocket watch from his jacket, he flipped the lid open and checked the time. The two women had been inside for longer than he deemed necessary.

He shook his head and clenched his jaw. The lass was going to test his every nerve. He could see it.

Stuffing the watch back into his pocket, he pushed off the carriage he'd been leaning against and made his way inside. He was getting ready to ring the bell to call for the innkeeper when commotion from the stairs caught his attention.

Lizzie, her maid close on her heels, descended the stairs as she spoke over her shoulder. "I dinna ken what he thinks will happen—"

"Miss!" Her maid snapped, nodding toward Malcolm.

Lizzie's head snapped to him, her mouth open in surprise, and missing the next step, she lost her footing.

As she began to tumble down, Malcolm rushed forward, catching her in his arms before she could crash onto the floor.

She slapped at his chest. "My lord. Please. Put me down at once. I insist."

He snapped his mouth shut to prevent him from saying something he would regret later and instead set her on her feet, making sure she had her balance before he let go.

"I do say, sir, ye are verra quick to put your hands where they dinna belong." She brushed her hands over her arms and then down the waist of her gown.

He raised a brow in her direction. "Well, then, Miss. Next time I will ensure to let ye fall, lest ye no' be subjected to my touch." He bent and snatched up the traveling bag she'd dropped in the process of her near fall and made for the door. The ride to Stonehaven was going to be long. He was calculating the trip in his mind to see if he could just push them straight through, knowing that it would be impossible.

Hands fisted on her hips, she scowled at him. "That is no' a nice thing to say."

Holding the door open, he waited for her to walk outside. "I dinna like to be accused of improper behavior when the intention was no' there. Believe me, if I had ill intent, ye would verra well ken." He raised his brows and locked eyes with her.

She harrumphed and stomped past him. Her maid hurried after her, keeping her eyes to the ground as she passed.

Lizzie waited by the carriage, her arms crossed in front of her ample bosom, tapping her foot impatiently.

"The weather appears to be cooperating." She tipped her face up to the sun, high in the sky.

It wasn't offering much warmth, but clear skies, though cool, were better than rain and wind.

He just grunted as he secured her bag to the carriage along with Mary's. The lass was vexing. He'd never been so twisted at a few sharp words from the fairer sex.

Offering his hand for both of the women to enter the carriage, he could only roll his eyes when Lizzie ignored his offering and he watched her wobble her way up the steps, barely keeping her balance.

Stubborn as a mule she was.

Well, two could play at that game.

With the door shut behind them, it wasn't lost on Malcolm that he would be spending many miles closed in this carriage with the two lasses.

Lizzie may be stubborn, pigheaded, and completely vexing to him as she glared at him from across the carriage. But all those things aside, her glare was beautiful. Her eyes, the color of chestnuts, had a beautiful almond shape to them. Her nose had the tiniest lift at the tip. Her full lips were ruby red and begging to be kissed.

He dragged his eyes away. If he kept thinking such thoughts the already long journey would be even longer. He didn't need to be pining over Lizzie Barclay, who could very well be a thief.

"How long until we stop next?" Lizzie asked.

"We've only just begun our journey. 'Twill be some time."

She sighed and focused her gaze on the trees beyond the window as they passed.

He'd had a conversation with Gunn before he'd left. His friend had warned him about what it would like for him to be traveling with the lass. She had her maid, which one could say could serve as chaperone, but even he understood that the visual was not the best. Him traveling with two lasses, confined to a carriage for days.

Gunn knew him well. He didn't worry that Malcolm's conduct would be ungentlemanly in anyway, but worried what it would look like to outward appearances.

The last thing he would do was compromise Lizzie in any way whatsoever. Being forced to marry because someone demanded so, was not anything that he had any interest in. Nor would he wish that upon the sulking woman sitting across from him.

He hadn't thought too much about marriage—other than he would probably never enter into such a union.

He was glad his friends had found happiness with their wives. He was thrilled for them, and they were truly happy whenever he saw them. The love they shared was evident on their faces.

But for him, love was not in the cards. He trusted no one outside of the friends he had grown up with. If the war had taught him anything, it was that ye only got hurt by the ones ye were trying to help.

He sighed, pushing his hands through his hair. Now that he thought about it, he was putting himself in a situation that he had vowed he never would again.

LIZZIE STOLE GLANCES of the earl when he wasn't looking. He seemed deep in thought and by the frown on his face, his thoughts weren't happy ones.

The crease in his forehead made him look much too serious. Her eyes met with Mary's who had been wringing her hands in her lap since they'd sat in the carriage.

She knew that the earl was irritated about having to travel to Stonehaven. It was evident by his countenance. And she should probably let him ride in silence, but she couldn't help herself.

"Sir," Lizzie called. "Do ye have my grandmama's jewelry on your person?"

His gaze slid over to her, and he cocked his head.

She found herself straightening at his assessment and she met his eyes, refusing to look away.

"Aye," he finally answered.

"May I see them, please?" It killed her to ask so nicely, when all she wanted to do was demand that he let her have them. She got the feeling that she would get her way easier with sweetness. The earl didn't seem the type to take orders very well. Nay, he was more the type to bark orders and expect everyone to obey.

He sighed and reached into his coat pocket, pulling out the necklace.

Mary gasped beside her.

"Ye did it, Miss. Ye really did find them," Mary whispered awestruck.

"I told ye I would, Mary. I was sure that Viscountess Wilson was the thief, and I was right."

The earl pulled back his hand, his brows furrowed.

"What did ye say?"

Lizzie thought back to what she had just said. "That I found my grandmama's jewelry?"

"Nay." He shook his head. "About the viscountess."

Lizzie went to speak and then snapped her mouth shut. Well, bother. She hadn't meant to say that in front of him.

"I, er, I dinna believe I made mention of the viscountess. Though she did put on a lovely party, did she no? The house decorations were magnificent."

"Do ye think I'm daft, Miss?"

He pierced her with a stare that she felt down to the tips of her toes.

"N-nay, my lord."

"Then dinna make me ask again."

She threw her hands up in defeat. "Fine. Ye will find out once we arrive at Tolton and ye see my grandmama's portrait wearing these verra jewels. With that evidence, obviously, I canna be the Phantom Prowler. That would be Viscountess Wilson."

"Ye should watch your tongue before accusing someone of such standing of thievery."

She didn't bother mentioning that he was doing the exact same thing to her. Though she didn't hold a standing such as the viscountess. "I agree, which is why I didna care to tell ye such. Ye insisted, might I remind ye."

Mary's quick intake of breath brought the dreaded realization that reminded Lizzie that she was speaking to an earl with such disrespect.

"I apologize, my lord. Sometimes my mouth gets ahead of my mind and says things it should no'."

He cocked his head to the side, his eyes narrowed as he studied her.

He shifted her grandmama's necklace from one hand to the other. The beads making a steady rhythm that was almost mesmerizing.

"Dinna apologize for speaking so bluntly. I must confess I find it refreshing. That aside, back to the viscountess."

Bother, she was hoping he would have dropped that after her change of subject. She watched as he played with the necklace, biting the inside of her cheek for her stupidity.

Realizing that she had no choice, she took a deep breath and flattened her palms on her skirt. "I believe, nay, I am certain, that Viscountess Wilson is the Phantom Prowler that has caught the attention of all of Scotland." She waited for him to strike out, but he just sat there, looking at her. Watching her.

"And that was confirmed when I found my grandmama's jewels in her chambers. The pieces had been stolen from my home some time ago at a ball my mama had hosted. The viscountess and her husband were in attendance."

"For certain there were many in attendance?"

"Aye." She nodded. "That is a true statement, my lord."

"Then how can ye be sure that the prowler is the viscountess? It makes no sense. She has no need for jewels."

"I do agree with ye, my lord. But I have researched extensively since the incident."

"Researched? Like investigated?" He chuckled. "This is priceless. Like the Bow Street Runners in London?"

She narrowed her eyes at him and crossed her arms. "Fine, dinna believe me. But then explain to me how my grandmama's jewels got in the viscountess's armoire in her chamber? And what of the viscountess's belongings? How is it that she has no' been affected by the robberies? I bet ye canna do that, can ye?"

"Miss," Mary warned beside her.

Lizzie jutted her chin out stubbornly. "I apologize, my lord." She rolled her lips together. "I only asked about the jewels because I wanted to hold them. 'Tis no' like I can run off with them. We are stuck inside a carriage."

He reached toward her and when she opened her palm, he dropped the necklace into her hand.

Lovingly, she trailed her fingertips over the gemstones. She could still see it hanging around her grandmama's slender neck, sparkling in the candlelight.

"Ye canna keep it. But ye can look at it for a few minutes."

The carriage hit a bump in the road and they all lurched to the side. The coachman shouted an apology and the carriage rambled along. By the time they reached Stonehaven, Lizzie predicted she would have a very sore rump indeed.

"Are ye alright?" the earl asked, concern creasing his forehead.

For a brief moment, she found his concern endearing. A quick glimpse of a softer side that he possessed underneath that gruff exterior.

"I am fine, thank ye. 'Twas just a bump."

He nodded. "A wee bit more than that to rock the carriage so. I can only hope it didn't damage anything. I dinna want any delays in our travels."

"My lord. Speaking of our travels. What exactly is your plan to get us to Stonehaven? Will we be stopping to rest often?"

He studied her as if trying to ascertain if she was genuinely curious or if she was asking questions to be difficult. She supposed some of her reasoning was to be a pain, but, in her defense, he deserved it for not believing her in the first place.

To accuse her of lying and of thievery...it was uncalled for. And in doing so, she didn't feel the need to placate him and go along with whatever plan he fostered up in his mind.

"Miss Barclay, we will stop as often as ye require," he finally answered. His look was challenging, as if he were daring her to complain about such liberties.

His gaze held hers and her stomach fluttered. He was a very handsome man. And his voice. Well, his voice was sweet as honeyed whisky whenever he spoke. It didn't matter if he was being curt or even accusing her of crimes. His voice slid over her skin and seeped into her pores, infiltrating all her senses. She broke eye contact and focused on the trees passing by, letting out a shuddering breath. Praying that he didn't see the effect he had on her.

How silly was she? To find the man that held her very life in his hands attractive? He held the key on whether she lived a free life or if she would spend her days in prison. She shuddered again but for an entirely different reason. Imagining herself locked away in the dungeons. Sustaining on bread and ale. The thought was depressing. The scenario also undeserving. She was innocent.

Never mind what it would do to her parents.

"What has your mind so occupied, Miss?"

Tilting her head, she wet her lips as she contemplated whether or not she should answer him. If they were in any other setting, her attitude would be frowned upon. She understood that. If her parents saw the way she was behaving, they would have her remanded to her room and not let out. But somehow, in this close setting, intimate almost, she felt like protocol was swept away and made obsolete. Because of that, she, once again, found herself unable to hold her tongue.

"Since ye are interested, my lord. I was ruminating on the fact that ye have for the lack of a better term, imprisoned my maid and I in your carriage, insisting that I am a thief. There is something verra wrong with ye." She crossed her arms defiantly and glared at the man sitting across from her.

A man, who infuriatingly, lifted his brow at her before barking out a laugh.

CHAPTER FIVE

MALCOLM COULDN'T HELP but laugh. He found Miss Barclay most comical. Aye, they were confined to this carriage, but truly, she could only blame herself for any situation she found herself in.

He gathered his wits and put on a serious face. Her scowl told him she didn't appreciate his reaction in any way whatsoever. "Might I remind ye that any situation ye now find yourself in is by your own doing?"

Her gaze slid to her maid before landing back on him. "Nay. Ye dinna." She raised an arched brow as she answered. "Ye have made it abundantly clear what ye think of me."

"I dinna think I have."

"Surely, ye jest, Sir. Ye have done naught but look upon me with suspicion."

He chuckled. "'Twas no' me that was caught elbow deep in the viscountess's chest of jewels. I was no' the one stealing that which doesna belong to me."

She sat forward, her hands clenched into tiny fists. "Those things do belong to me!" She held up the necklace and shook it in the air. "This belongs to me. I dinna ken how many times I need to tell ye. They are my grandmama's. Well, were, but that's beside the point. They belong to my family. They're mine to keep."

The lass was so defiant in her argument, it was hard to believe that she wasn't telling the truth. But he couldn't wrap his head around the story that she wove. The viscountess being the thief? That made no sense. Why would a woman of wealth risk so much for something she didn't need?

Now, Miss Barclay? Who kenned if Tolton Hall even existed? She could be leading him on a wild goose chase into the Highlands. What her end game could be, he hadn't the slightest idea.

But say she was telling the truth, what did that mean for the viscountess? Had she been given the jewelry? How else could she explain how she came into possession of jewelry that was stolen from the Barclay home?

It was a wicked web being weaved. Malcolm wasn't sure he wanted to be a part of it. And as frustrating as Miss Barclay was, he still found her entertaining in her defiance.

"Say they are yours. Why were they at the Wilsons'?"

She blew out an exasperated breath, throwing her hands up in the air. "I dinna ken how many times I need to explain the same thing to ye," she said, her voice low in irritation. "She stole them from my family."

He shook his head. "I dinna believe it. What would be her reasoning?"

Miss Barclay shrugged her shoulders. "I dinna ken. Mayhap she thought they were pretty." She held up the necklace and looked at it admiringly. "Ye have to agree 'tis a beautiful piece."

His throat was suddenly dry. The look of pure adoration on her face had Malcolm once again questioning his reconnaissance skills. He'd uncovered spies and traitors for the crown for Christ's sake. Could this woman sitting across from him demanding her innocence be pulling the wool over his eyes?

Mayhap he was blinded by her beauty, which was most definitely impossible to ignore. Her honeysuckle perfume filled the interior of the carriage and tickled his nose. A pleasant scent that fit her well. With each breath she took, her chest heaved, causing her breasts to lift and he found himself having to continuously avert his gaze, lest he find himself, scooting to his knees in front of her and burying his face in her soft curves.

He shook his head trying to clear the erotic images prancing about like they were the only thing he needed to think about. He'd be damned if he let this woman bring him to his knees. He'd never let anyone else have such a hold on him, he sure as hell wouldn't let this one.

"Tell me, my lord. Are ye married?"

"Pardon?" That was indeed a quick shift into an entirely different topic of conversation. Right away, he knew she was trying to draw his attention away from her thievery. He'd allow it for now, but he wasn't so sure this was the best conversation to be had considering his thoughts.

"A wife? Is there a Lady Kennedy waiting for ye at home? I would hate to ken what she is thinking about ye traveling with a maiden. Alone, I might add."

It was his turn to scowl at her implication. "We arena alone." He dipped his head in Mary's direction. "Your maid is here. Alas, I havena a wife." Nor did he want one. He was perfectly happy single. Free to bed who he wanted, when he wanted. Which wasn't to say he hadn't had a lass or two try to trick him into marriage. He had. Obviously, they had been unsuccessful, and he had no interest in being saddled to a woman.

Even a beauty such as Miss Barclay. Although a quick romp wasn't something he would reject if it were offered. He belonged to no one and planned to keep it that way.

"Surely someone as braw as ye has had many marriage prospects, nay?"

He schooled his features, uncomfortable with her line of inquiries. "And what of ye? Are ye no' of marrying age. Certainly by now ye have been introduced into Society. Why have ye no' married? Or do ye have a husband waiting for ye back in Stonehaven?"

"I most certainly do no'," she snapped. "There isna anyone who has asked me."

He chortled. "I bet. Your countenance would scare off any man looking for a wife."

She gasped. "Ye, sir, are verra rude." She straightened in her seat, pressing her lips so tightly together they turned white as she avoided his eyes. "My parents are in no hurry for me to marry," she finally added.

"Or," he drawled, "they've been unsuccessful in finding a match that will put up with your smart tongue."

Her mouth rounded in shock. "Ye canna speak to me in such a way. I thought titled men of the upper echelons of society were well-mannered. Ye, sir, are the exact opposite."

"Miss," Mary whispered sharply. "Mind your words," she warned.

"Me? Mary, please. Ye have heard how he's spoken to me. He's been rude since we first met."

"With good reason."

"Says who?"

And they'd circled back around to the reason they found themselves confined in this carriage. He was growing tired of the redundancy.

"I suggest we hold our tongues for some time and enjoy the ride." He reached into his pocket and drew out some papers he had to review, effectively dismissing the lass.

Something she wasn't happy about judging by the way she harrumphed and once again folded her arms on her chest. Every time she did so, she drew more attention to her bosom and he fought the urge to stare.

"I can see why ye arena married." She broke the silence that had lasted for less than a minute.

Damn, the lass liked to yammer.

He said naught. Only looked at her as he waited for her to continue, which she surely would.

"Aye. Ye are crude and your demeanor is most unwelcoming. A woman wants to be loved, not regarded as a nuisance, which is most certainly how ye would treat her." She sat back, glaring at him, with a smirk lifting the corners of her mouth.

She was purposely trying to rile him. He would not fall for her antics.

"Marriage isna always about love. More oft than no' 'tis about business. Surely your parents must have explained this to ye. Unfortunately for ye, even coin canna save ye, which is why ye find yourself still on the marriage mart."

"Ugh, ye are truly incorrigible. Has anyone e'er told ye that?"

He shrugged. "Mayhap a time or two. But I must note, that ye didna deny my assessment."

She turned in her seat, facing the window, and doing her best to give him her back. Mary hid her smile behind her hand as she patted Miss Barclay's shoulder.

"Mayhap 'tis a good idea to try to rest your eyes, Miss. We still have a long journey ahead before we stop."

Malcolm listened for her answer, but Miss Barclay for once, remained silent.

He had thought that was what he wanted, but he found he missed her obstinance. He had enjoyed their banter. He found the way she refused to bow down to him refreshing.

It affected him in a most unexpected way. And he wasn't sure what to do with the feelings that were running rampant through his head right now.

LIZZIE ABHORRED LONG carriage rides. It was why she usually passed the time in idle chitchat. Something the earl obviously did not find favor in.

He'd been reading the papers he'd plucked out of his pocket for what seemed like hours, the only sound was the carriage wheels as they bounced over the gravel of the road.

She hid a yawn behind her hand and wondered how much longer it would be before they stopped for a rest. The number of times she'd had to bite her lip to stop from talking were too many to count.

Unable to take the silence anymore, she spoke up. "My lord. Can we stop soon? I find my legs in need of a stretch."

Lord Kennedy looked at her over the edge of his papers, his brow cocked up as he pondered her question.

"I suppose ye are right, Miss." He knocked on the carriage wall, alerting the coachman to stop.

Once the carriage rocked to a halt, the door swung open.

"My lord?" the coachman asked.

"Aye. The ladies need a brief respite to stretch their legs and take care of personal matters. Any concerns?"

The man shook his head. "Nay, my lord."

The earl nodded and stepped out of the carriage, turning and offering her his hand. "Miss Barclay."

She accepted his offer, the heat of his hand sending bolts of warmth up her arm. As annoying as she found her, her…what was he? Her host? Her guardian? Nay, her jailor. As annoying as she found her jailor, she couldn't tamp down her body's reaction every time they touched.

With Mary by her side, she looked around at her surroundings. Thick pine trees lined either side of the road. Storm clouds were moving in and she expected before long they would be riding through inclement weather.

"Great," she mumbled under her breath and stomped around the carriage toward the trees.

"Dinna wander far, Miss," the earl ordered.

She straightened. Something in the way he barked out commands, as if she were a soldier, irked her. Grating on her nerves. Just because he thought her a thief didn't mean that he could take over every minute of her life.

"We will be far enough to afford us some privacy. Your coachman said 'tis a safe spot. We will be fine. Come, Mary." She grasped Mary's hand and pulled her along. A few feet into the woods and when she turned around, she could barely see the carriage.

They could run and easily get lost in the trees. It would be an option if she knew where they were. Alas, she hadn't a clue, so running wasn't an option. But the thought remained in her mind. If the opportunity presented itself, she would run in a heartbeat. She still had her grandmama's necklace. She only needed to get the earl to hand over the earrings as well. Once she had possession of both, there was no reason why she shouldn't try to escape his clutches.

"Miss, I dinna think we should stray too far from the road. We will ne'er find our way out."

Mary was right, of course, but Lizzie's rebellious side was tempted to see how far she could go or how long she could be gone before the earl came looking for them.

A roar of thunder rumbled through the air. She jumped at the sound and all thoughts of running left her mind. She hated the thunder. Always had. Ever since she was a young child.

Another rumble and she gathered her skirts. "Mary, let us make haste and get back to the shelter of the carriage afore the storm catches us out here."

"Aye, Miss."

They hurried through relieving themselves and quickly made their way back.

The earl stood on the edge of the road waiting for them to emerge. As they did, a bolt of lightning cracked nearby, and Lizzie yelped as she jumped.

Concern etched his handsome face as he hurried her into the carriage, and then Mary before climbing in himself.

Rain came pounding down on the roof of the carriage and the skies grew dark.

"Damn it," the earl cursed before looking at her sheepishly. "Pardon my crass words, Miss."

The thunder boomed and she cried out again, grasping for Mary's hand and clenching it tightly.

"Are ye all right?" he asked, brows drawn together in worry.

She was shivering and he quickly removed his jacket and placed it on her shoulders. His spicy scent enveloped her. Something she would have savored if she weren't on the verge of panic.

"'Tis just a storm, Miss. 'Twill pass quickly."

"Miss Barclay doesna care for storms o'ermuch," Mary explained as she rubbed her hand up and down Lizzie's back, trying to calm her nerves.

"I can see that. It came on quickly, let us hope that it clears out as quick."

Lightning lit up the interior of the carriage and she shrunk back.

She could feel the earl's eyes on her, studying her. He must think her a fool for her reaction. He more than likely thought her juvenile in her reaction.

"Did ye have a bad experience with a storm, Lass?" he queried.

She had. When she was very young. She remembered traveling with her parents when a storm had taken them unawares. They were outside. In a forest. The lightning hit a tree close to them, causing it to split and fall, landing on her father, crushing his leg.

She could still hear his cry of pain. Her mother's scream of fear as she called out for help. But they were walking alone. Lizzie had to run back to Tolton Hall for help. Her brother had been visiting relatives so he hadn't been there to help.

Their gardener and stable boys ran to her when she came scream-ing through the grounds. With their strength they were able to lift the tree off her father's leg and carry him back home where they called for the physician.

Her father still walked with a slight limp to this day. The whole experience was traumatic, and every storm brought her back to that feeling of helplessness. She'd thought she'd lost her father that day.

Unable to stop shaking, she just nodded her head.

The earl moved onto his knees in front of her, taking her hands in his and forcing her to look at him. "Lass, I promise ye. Naught will happen to ye. We are safe."

Another flash of lightning followed by a loud boom of thunder caused her to jump and she couldn't hold back a scream.

Immediately, he gathered her in his strong arms, and sat her on his lap. He rocked them back and forth, stroking his fingers up and down her back as he told her everything would be fine. She buried her face in his chest, not caring that what they were doing was wrong. She just wanted to feel safe.

He began singing softly, his deep voice soothing as he sang the words with such emotion she couldn't help but concentrate on him.

The sound of him.

The feel of him.

The scent of him.

Just him.

CHAPTER SIX

MALCOLM USUALLY WASN'T one for singing, especially to a beautiful lass, but here he was. Singing to Miss Barclay, whilst she sat on his lap, wrapped in his arms, as she struggled to calm down.

Singing was the first thing that popped into his mind when he'd picked up her trembling body. He didn't know many songs, but this was one he'd taken a particular fancy to and remembered all the words. As his hands stroked her back and his voice filled the carriage, the rain offering a rhythmic backdrop, his only worry was to ease her nerves.

The way she buried her face in his chest, her hands clenched into tiny fists, his body was having an awakening of its own.

Mary watched his every movement from the seat across from them. Her forehead creased in concern. Whether it was due to his actions or worry for her mistress, he wasn't certain. But she remained quiet as she watched, wringing her hands in her lap.

He reckoned something bad had happened to Lizzie for her to have such a reaction to the storm, but he didn't want to press her when she was so distraught. He only wanted to offer her comfort. To show her that she was safe with him.

That voice in the back of his mind broke into his thoughts. Reminding him she was a thief. This was work. A mission he'd been assigned.

But he ignored the voice of reason. The one that also reminded him that he had no right to be holding her so tightly in his arms. She shouldn't be in his arms at all.

Never mind on his lap.

Even though she fit perfectly.

The carriage ambled along, a bit slower now that the roads were muddy from the heavy rain. He hoped they didn't get stuck, but that was entirely plausible considering the storm.

Thankfully, the thunder and lightning had ceased, and now it was just rain.

He should let her go. Set her back on her seat to sit by her maid.

But he couldn't. He found himself enjoying the feel of her in his arms too much.

Mary was watching them closely. He didn't blame the maid. It was her duty to ensure her lady was safe and not compromised. Something that he was surely making difficult.

Malcolm would never do anything to mar the lass's reputation. No matter how much his body screamed right now. He could only hope that the lass wouldn't notice his reaction. He was almost uncomfortably hard. The urge to rearrange himself to be more discreet was there, but he didn't want to disturb the lass. And he feared doing so would only bring attention to his predicament.

She had finally stopped trembling. That was a good sign.

Pushing away from his chest, she looked up at him, her cheeks tinged pink as she patted his shirt.

"I-I apologize, my lord. I am no' one to act in such a manner. 'Twas a bit of an embarrassing show, I must admit."

He tucked his finger under her chin and forced her eyes to his. "Dinna apologize, Miss. How are ye feeling now?"

Her gaze moved to the window, taking in the lightening sky, and nodded. "I am much improved, Sir. Thank ye."

She moved across the carriage to sit beside Mary once again, who clasped her hands in hers and brought them to her lap.

Quickly, he adjusted his sitting position to not give the women a fright. Had he been anyplace else, with any other company, he would have taken her right then and there in the carriage as they ambled down the road on the way to their destination. Well, once she regained her wits.

He usually didn't hold back when it came to his body's urges. Of course, the women he had bedded were always willing participants. He wasn't a sod. Forcing a woman to do something she did not want to do was not something he found pleasure in. He was far from innocent, but he had his ethics.

Right now he was praising himself on his control. Soon, they should arrive at the inn where they would sup and spend the night.

And a long night it would be. He wouldn't sleep in their room. That would no doubt spread rumors that didn't need to be spread, but he would sleep close to ensure their safety.

And to make sure they didn't chance an escape. He doubted they would, but just in case.

But he figured as long as he had possession of her grandmother's jewels, she wouldn't run. She still held on to the necklace she'd asked for earlier. But the earrings remained in his pocket. The chances of her running off in the middle of the night were slim. She wanted to make sure she regained ownership of her family's jewelry.

That is if they were truly hers.

Time would only tell.

THE CARRIAGE CAME to a stop, rocking them to and fro. They'd finally arrived at their destination for the night.

Inside the inn, Malcolm spoke to the owner manning the desk and secured two rooms, across the hall from each other, and escorted Lizzie and Mary to theirs.

Lizzie looked around, taking in the room. Her face gave away no inclination as to whether or not she thought it a proper room for them to stay.

"Will this suffice, Miss?" He asked. If she didn't find the room appealing, he would talk to the innkeeper to see if something different was available.

She nodded and gave him a small smile. "'Tis just fine, my lord."

The space held one large bed. Lizzie and Mary would have to share, but neither of the lasses complained about that so he figured it probably wasn't the first time they'd been in such a scenario.

"I'll leave ye two to get ready for dinner. I shall come by to get ye in an hour if that is acceptable?"

"Aye. That will be perfect. Thank ye, my lord."

Her eyes were still a bit red and puffy from the tears she'd shed during the storm, but she appeared to be back to her normal demeanor.

Nodding, he backed out of the room and closed the door behind him and made his way to his own room.

Sitting on the bed, he cradled his head in his hands and wondered once again what he had gotten himself into. With a heavy sigh, he moved to the basin, he splashed cool water on his face and wiped it dry with the towel hanging from the hook on the side of the table.

He hoped they wouldn't have to endure any more storms on their way to Stonehaven. A repeat of this afternoon wasn't something he wanted to see again. Moreover, he wasn't sure Lizzie's nerves could take it. He had never seen anyone so deathly afraid of storms before. The pure terror in her eyes was tragic.

Never mind himself. Because if she had that same reaction to another storm, he knew he wouldn't be able to stop himself from pulling her into his arms again and cradling her even tighter as he kissed all her worries away.

"Fuck," he mumbled into the empty room. "She's a thief, Kennedy." He had to keep reminding himself of that fact. He could only imagine where his mind would take him.

Even as he said the words, he was having difficulty believing them. The lass was far too meek and the amount of noise she was making whilst rummaging through the viscountess's armoire gave her innocence away. There was no scenario where she could get away with all the crimes she'd done with being so careless. Certainly, she would have been caught before now.

Based off the articles he'd read, he believed that the thief was more than likely a man.

However, catching the lass red-handed led some credence to Lizzie being the actual prowler.

It would be interesting to see once they arrived at Tolton Hall if the lass could prove her innocence or if she'd just taken him on a fool's ride. Hopefully, he was smarter than that.

Putting his trust in the wrong person had burned him before. Memories of Angus assaulted him. He'd believed that lad was true to their country, never once suspecting him for the spy amongst their ranks.

Aye, he'd caught him in the end, but he should have seen what was right under his nose much sooner than he had.

And the image of watching Angus hang was an image he could never erase from his mind.

Malcolm dropped back down on the bed, leaning his elbows on his knees and stared at the floor. He hated the melancholy that filled him whenever he thought of Angus. The guilt he felt even though he'd only done his duty.

But it still hurt. He took in a few deep breaths, slowly pushing them out through his mouth. With each breath out he forced a memory to leave his body with it.

These bouts of sadness and regret didn't overtake him often anymore, but there were still times where they snuck into his mind, causing him to remember and reminding him not to give his trust to anyone.

LIZZIE COLLAPSED ONTO the bed and groaned as soon as the earl closed the door. The bed was surprisingly soft and she sunk into the thick coverlet.

She scrubbed at her face thinking about her predicament.

"Mary, what have I done?"

"Miss?" Her maid, who had been setting out Lizzie's items for the night, paused and turned to her. "Whate'er are ye referring to?"

"Can ye imagine Mama and Papa's reaction when we arrive back home with the earl in tow?" She sat up and crossed her legs. "Ne'er mind that we traveled with him *alone* all the way back from Tywnholm. They'll also find out that I wasna visiting my friend. This is just one big mess."

Mary put down the night chemise she'd withdrawn from Lizzie's bag and sat down beside her, patting her leg.

"Dinna fash, Miss. Ye're parents have always been most understanding."

Lizzie shook her head. "No' about this. I lied, Mary. They willna take kindly to that."

Mary sighed, worry creasing her forehead.

Lizzie grasped her hands in hers. She knew what her maid was thinking. If Lizzie was going to pay the price for her disobedience, Mary would surely be punished as well for allowing it to happen.

"I promise ye, Mary. Naught will happen to ye. I will make sure of it. Ye only did this because I tricked ye into it. Lord kens, my parents understand me well enough. They'll ken I left ye no choice. Ye needna fash."

Mary gave her a small smile, but it didn't reach her eyes. Lizzie was overcome with guilt with the realization that her actions could very well have dire consequences for Mary. But she meant her promises to her maid and planned to keep them. She would not let her lose her employment due to something that Lizzie made her do.

"Are ye hungry?" Lizzie asked brightly, hoping the change of subject would lighten the mood. "Let us get ready to eat. I dinna want to keep the earl waiting." She lowered her voice as if he could hear them through the door and across the hall. "I've a feeling that he doesna appreciate tardiness."

They both giggled and fell back on the bed together, staring at the ceiling.

"'Tis thoughtful of the earl to take the journey back to Stonehaven slow. That must mean he believes ye, aye?"

Lizzie sighed. "I dinna ken. I am no' so certain he believes me, but it does seem that he is giving us some leeway by no' rushing us back."

Mary pushed herself off the bed and pulled Lizzie with her.

"Come on, Miss. Let us make ye presentable for the earl."

"Mary," she exclaimed. "Dinna jest with such things. I will be presentable for dinner, no' for the earl."

Mary lifted an eyebrow. "I am no' blind, Miss. I see the way ye look at the man. He is quite handsome, I must admit. Even if he is a wee bit gruff."

"Dinna forget he also thinks I'm a thief." She laughed in disbelief. "Can ye imagine, Mary? Me as the Phantom Prowler? 'Tis comical to say the least. I could ne'er pull off such heists."

"Truer words ye have ne'er muttered, Miss. Ye couldna e'en pull off this one." Mary chuckled as she stuck her head in the wardrobe. "Have ye any preferences on what to wear this eve?"

Lizzie shook her head. "If I havena been in this gown for so long, I would just stay as is, but I dinna think that would be proper." She got up and looked at her dress choices. "How about this one?" She pointed to a light-blue gown adorned with ivory-colored lace.

Mary nodded and began to work her magic. Once she was dressed, they moved onto her hair. After a badly needed brushing, Mary twisted it into a tight chignon and secured it with a ribbon that matched the blue of her dress.

"Happy?" Mary asked as she looked at her in the reflection of the looking glass.

"Once again, Mary, ye have managed a miracle." She spun in the chair. "'Tis another reason my parents willna reprieve ye of your position. I need ye too much."

Her maid smiled and this time, her eyes brightened with the gesture.

Lizzie really did not want Mary making herself sick of the possibility of losing her job. Her parents could be angered with her all they wanted, but she wouldna allow them to take out their frustrations on poor Mary.

A sharp knock sounded, and Lizzie jumped. "Miss Barclay," the earl called from the hall. "Are ye ladies ready for dinner?"

Mary approached the door but looked at Lizzie before opening it, only doing so when Lizzie gave her a nod to do so.

"My lord." Mary dipped into a curtsy when she swung the door open.

Lizzie did the same and when she lifted her head and looked at the earl, her breath hitched in her throat. He looked devastatingly dashing in his deep-green waistcoat and white ruffled shirt. Black breeches hugged his muscular thighs and Lizzie felt scandalous just noticing that fact.

"Shall we?"

She snapped her eyes to his face, and cleared her throat, nodding. "Aye, my lord."

He offered his arm, and she took it. The contact sending frissons throughout her body. He smelled divine. As if he'd taken the best parts of the sea and the forest and blended them together to make the most satisfying scent.

Mary followed them closely as they descended the stairs and made their way to the dining hall. Even with the ire of Lizzie's parents hanging over her head, her maid fulfilled her duty of chaperone. Lizzie was certain that would be one of the first questions her parents asked. Along with all of the obvious questions of course.

As they made their way downstairs, the most delicious aromas assaulted Lizzie's senses. Her stomach grumbled embarrassingly, and she covered it with her hand as if the action would make the noise cease.

Beside her, the earl chuckled. "We will satisfy your hunger shortly, Lass."

She liked when he called her lass. It did weird things to her stomach. That one simple word had way more of an impact on her than when he called her miss. It was almost as if it were more intimate.

Intimate.

She should not be thinking such thoughts of the person that could have her thrown in prison for the rest of her life. Or have her hand for stealing.

How daft did she have to be to grow feelings for the very person that held her life in his hands.

Even if those hands were very large. Very strong. Very capable.

What would it feel like to be wrapped in his warm embrace? An embrace that wasn't prefaced by her having a fit of panic due to a storm.

Nay. A real embrace. One filled with passion, perhaps?

She almost mewled at the thought and cleared her throat to cover her reaction.

The earl looked down at her, curiosity crinkling his eyes, but he said naught as they were shown to the table and he pulled out the chair for her to sit.

Thanking him, she quickly took a sip from the glass of wine set in front of her.

'Twas going to be a long dinner.

CHAPTER SEVEN

W AS IT POSSIBLE for dinner to be an erotic experience? If one had asked Malcolm before this eve he would have said absolutely not.

But sitting across from the beautiful Lizzie Barclay, watching her enjoy her meal with such fervor, it most certainly was. Especially when she moaned with delight as she sank her teeth into the berry tart that was served for dessert.

He found himself clearing his throat and straightening himself in his chair more times than he wanted to admit.

Their conversation was easy. Natural.

As if they were long-time acquaintances.

"Have ye always lived in Stonehaven?"

She licked her lips, picking up a crumb from the tart that had settled on them, and nodded. "Aye. My papa was born there and my mama was from Inverness. Of course, when they married, they settled into Papa's familial home, Tolton Hall. 'Tis a beautiful estate as ye will see." Her eyes clouded before she quickly guarded her gaze and took another bite of the tart.

"Ye said your grandmama has passed."

She frowned and her gaze dipped down to her plate.

"Aye."

"I am verra sorry to hear that. Is your grandfather still with ye?"

Lizzie shook her head. The baubles in her ears swinging from side to side. "Nay. I ne'er kenned him. He passed before I was born. 'Tis why my grandmama lived with us."

He nodded. Malcolm could understand the loss of family before ye met them. He'd been in much the same situation. He had never met his grandparents either. From either side. And his parents died when he was very young. So young that he didn't remember them.

He'd been raised by nannies and tutors, preparing him to become the best earl he could be. Which he hoped he succeeded in and was making his parents proud. At least he liked to think that they would be proud to see the man he'd become.

"What about ye?" she asked, drawing his attention back to her. "Is Twynholm your home?"

"Nay. I do have an estate near there, but 'tis no' where I spend verra much of my time. I usually stay in Culzean Castle."

Her eyes rounded at the word castle.

"I have always found castles fascinating. Aye, we have our estates, but castles hold so much more history than an estate."

"I must confess, I do enjoy my time at Culzean. Though it can be monotonous at times."

She cocked her head to the side, a small frown on her face. "How so?"

He shrugged. "The days are always the same. The same tasks need to be done. There is a definite lack of excitement to poring over the finances day after day."

"What do ye like to do for excitement?"

That question caught him unawares. He took a long pull of wine and set the glass on the table before thrumming his fingers against the cloth-covered wood. "'Tis a good question, Miss. I find since I returned from the war, I havena really done much that would qualify for excitement."

Her eyes flared. "Ye fought in the war?"

"Aye. I have been home for a few years now. But that experience never leaves ye."

"Ye are lucky to have made it home. No' e'eryone was such."

A faraway look entered her eyes, and Malcolm had the feeling that she had known someone who fought.

"War is ne'er fun and ne'er something to be taken lightly. I did what I had to do for our country and enjoyed my job while there, no matter how difficult it was."

She nodded. "What was your job?"

He continued to tap his fingers on the table as he studied her face, wondering how much he should tell her. Deciding to downplay what he did, he answered. "Information gathering, mostly." It wasn't a complete lie.

"My brother served, but unfortunately he didna make it home." Sadness caused the corners of her mouth to slope down into a frown and her eyes to mist over.

"I am verra sorry, Lass." Without thinking, he reached across the table and grasped her hand in his, rubbing his thumb over her knuckle in an offering of comfort.

She pulled back her hand as if she'd been scorched and quickly looked around the room.

He cursed under his breath.

Bloody hell. He had meant naught by the gesture, but also understood what the ramifications of such an action could mean for a young lass.

"I apologize. Both for my actions and for your brother."

She cleared her throat and pushed back from the table.

He hurried to stand.

"I wish to return to my room for the night, my lord. Thank ye for the conversation." She spun on her heel and rushed from the room, Mary following closely on her heels.

He looked to the ceiling and shook his head, disgusted with himself. He called for a servant and when she approached, he asked, "Whisky?"

"Aye, my lord." The serving maid bowed and scuttled off. She returned a few minutes later with a decanter of whisky and a glass.

He offered his thanks and poured himself a generous serving.

Knocking back the deep-amber liquid, he hissed at the burn as it made its way down his throat. He refilled the glass but this time, nursed his drink.

He had a duty to protect the lass and her maid. And to keep an eye on her to ensure she didn't attempt to escape. Though he really didn't think she would do that. After all, she'd already given him the name of the estate where she resided. If she tried to run, that's where she would go, and he would just follow.

Either way, he needed to keep his wits about him this night.

He finished the glass and bid good eve to the serving maid and the innkeeper as he passed the man hunched over a logbook on the desk.

Upstairs, he paused outside Lizzie's door and listened. He could hear voices but couldn't discern the conversation. That was fine. He just wanted to ensure they were inside.

Inside his own room, he washed up for the night, but he had no plans on sleeping in this room on the bed that would no doubt be more comfortable than the floor.

Nay, he would be posted out in the hall. He told himself it was to make sure the lass didn't make a run for home, but he kenned deep inside it was because he wanted to ensure the lass's safety.

He would make sure no man entered the room while two young women slept inside.

LIZZIE AWOKE IN the middle of the night and tossed and turned for some time, unable to fall back to sleep. Whenever this happened, the only thing she found that would help was a glass of warm milk. Obviously, she didn't have any in her room, and after a few moments of worrying about what the innkeeper would think about her going down to the kitchen for a glass, she decided that if she wanted to get any sleep at all this night, she didn't have a choice.

Slipping quietly out of bed, being careful not to awaken Mary, she pushed her feet into slippers and wrapped herself in a robe. She looked over her shoulder as she pulled the door open, saying a silent prayer that the hinges didn't squeak, and stepped into the hall.

"Where are ye going lass?"

"Christ!" She exclaimed before she could stop it. "Ye frightened me. What are ye doing in the hall?"

Sitting on the floor, his back against his room's door, sat the earl, his arm resting on a bent knee, a smirk tilting his mouth.

"Making sure ye arena escaping," he said quietly.

She threw her arms up in the air. "Surely, ye jest, Sir." She tapped her palm on her chest, trying to calm her beating heart. She feared it would beat right out of her chest at how much he made her jump. "If I were planning an escape, which I am no', but if I were, would I be wearing slippers and a robe?"

She crossed her arms and pierced him with a stare.

He shrugged. "Mayhap no', but one can ne'er ken." He pushed himself up to his feet, towering over her. "Why are ye out in the hall in your nightclothes?"

Her cheeks heated as his eyes traveled slowly down her body and she cinched her robe tighter.

"I canna sleep. I am after a glass of warm milk."

"I can help ye with that."

"Nay, I can go to the kitchen on my own, thank ye." She couldn't even imagine the rumors that would spread if they were seen together in the middle of the night. Her in her nightclothes and no chaperone anywhere in sight.

"I insist."

She looked back and forth down the hall. No one was about. The chances of them being caught were slim. Everyone should be asleep in their beds, which is where she wished she was. The sooner she could get some milk, the sooner she would be.

"Fine," she huffed, heading toward the stairs.

The earl followed silently behind her, holding a lantern he'd grabbed from a table in the hall. How someone so massive could be so quiet, she had no idea. She thought about him sleeping in the hall. Was he really doing that to ensure she stayed put? It seemed excessive to her. Overbearing even.

"The kitchen is this way." At the bottom of the stairs, he took her elbow and led her to the left.

The soft glow of the lantern lit their way, casting shadows on the walls as they padded quietly down the hall.

Thankfully the kitchen was empty when they entered. She watched as the earl found a jug of milk and grabbed a saucepan and set it on the stove. After he poured in some milk, he lit the flame to warm the milk and turned toward her.

"Have a seat, Lass." He pointed to a chair at a small table that Lizzie assumed was where the cook sat when she needed a respite or to eat.

She sat as instructed. The care he was showing for her took her by surprise. One minute he was gruff and the next he was making her a glass of warm milk, sweet as ever.

"Do ye have a wife, my lord?" The question was out of her mouth before she even thought of what she was asking. It also wouldn't be abnormal for him to be married. He was titled, attentive, caring, and handsome. She hadn't been around many men what she presumed to be his age, but it seemed that those were traits that he would attain with a wife.

"Ye asked me that earlier, before the storm. But, nay, I dinna, Lass. And, please, stop calling me lord or sir. Malcolm is fine."

"My apologies." She flushed at the repeated question. She had completely forgotten she had posed the question earlier. It was just when she saw him being so thoughtful and caring, she found it inconceivable that he was unmarried.

Cocking her head to the side, she studied him as he stirred the milk with a wooden spoon he'd snatched from a utensil holder. It didn't feel right to call him by his given name. It felt too personal. They were not close acquaintances. Nor friends. Most definitely not. Right now, she was pretty much in his custody.

"'Twouldna be proper for me to do so. Sisters then?"

"Nay. What are ye fishing for, Lass?"

She lifted a brow in surprise. She was certain he'd learned his behavior from a female in his life, but it appears she was wrong. His mama could have taught him so well, she supposed. His ire at her questions was interesting. Was he trying to hide something from her?

"I am no' fishing for anything, S-er, Malcolm." It felt odd to her to address him as such. She wasn't sure if she liked it or not.

"If ye are no' looking for information than why the barrage of questions regarding my relationships?"

She folded her hands in her lap, rolling her fingers together. "I just thought I would like to ken ye. It appears that we will be spending at least a few days in each other's company. I was only trying to find common ground betwixt us."

He turned off the flame and poured the milk into a mug before handing it to her.

"Thank ye." She blew at the liquid before testing the temperature with a tentative sip. It was perfect. She should have known. It seemed the earl—Malcolm—could do no wrong.

"Whilst I agree our time together will be lengthy, I dinna think 'tis a good idea for us to get too personal."

"Well, I do apologize for prying. I was only trying to be cordial. I shall refrain from doing so in future conversations," she snapped.

Leaning against the counter, he sighed, pushing his hands through his honey hair.

"How is your milk?" he asked.

"'Tis perfect. Thank ye."

He nodded and looked quickly away.

Malcolm Kennedy was surely a mystery. The question that needed to be answered was if it was a mystery she wanted to solve.

CHAPTER EIGHT

MALCOLM KNEW THAT the lass was only trying to make idle conversation and that she wasn't really prying into his history and personal life.

But when she sat in front of him in her night robe, the material much too thin to be proper, he had a hard time not reacting to the lass. He could see the swell of her breasts, the hard peaks of her nipples poking the fabric.

His cock jumped to attention as if it were answering a battle cry and it was taking all of his self-control to not pull her up from her chair, wrap her in his arms, and capture her mouth like an invading army.

Over and over in his mind he had to remind himself she wasn't some lass he picked up on the street. She was potentially a criminal. A thief who had stolen items from some of the biggest estates across Scotland.

"Malcolm?"

His name on her lips was a sweet song and he wondered what it would sound like for her to say it with her voice husky with passion.

He rubbed his hands across his face, trying to erase the erotic imagery trampling through his mind.

"Aye?"

She stood and brought the mug over to the basin of water to wash it before taking a towel to dry it before replacing it back in the cupboard.

"I feel much better and would like to return to my room."

"Of course." He grabbed the lantern and waved his hand for her to exit the kitchen. It was selfish of him, but he wanted to watch her arse rock from side to side as she ascended the stairs in front of him. And when he did, he had to swallow the groan that wanted to escape him at the sight.

Mayhap he should look for a wench to get lost in for the night. But just the thought soured his stomach. Nay, a wench wouldn't do. It wasn't that he just needed the release. There was only one person that could cure what he was longing for, and it was someone he could not touch.

At the door to her room, she spun and pierced him with a serious look. "Are ye going to sleep in the hall for the rest of the night."

"Aye."

Her brows furrowed. "Go sleep in your bed. I promise ye that Mary and I will still be here in the morn."

"That is what a thief would say," he jested with a wink.

She sucked in a sharp breath. "Ye tease."

"I do," he chuckled. "I shall think about where I will sleep. Rest well, Lass."

She paused for a moment longer and he didn't think she was going to enter the room, but finally she nodded.

"Good night, my lord," she whispered before disappearing inside.

He leaned against his own door, staring at the door she'd just shut quietly behind her, clenching his jaw. There was no question that she and her maid would be there in the morn. He had no doubt that she wouldn't run. She was quite genuine when she'd made the proclamation.

But he couldn't protect her if he was sleeping in his room.

Out here, he could see everyone that walked down the corridor. No one in their right mind would attempt to enter the ladies' room whilst he was here so once again, he sat down and leaned his back against the door to his room.

The lasses would be safe. He would make certain of it.

The rest of the night passed with no events of note. As the sun rose and weak rays filtered in through the window at the end of the hall, Malcolm stood and groaned at the pain that shot through his back. These days his body much preferred sleeping on a soft mattress instead of the hard floor. The aches would only be more pronounced after another day stuck crammed into a carriage as they continued their journey to Stonehaven.

He listened at the door of Lizzie's room and could hear shuffling inside. The hum of the rustle of the inn coming to life reached his ears, and satisfied that no one would attempt any harm to the lasses in the light of day with people milling about, he ducked inside his own room.

The bed was soft as he sat on it, his body begging him to lie down for just a bit. He fought the urge to just close his eyes for a minute. Instead, he walked over to the basin and splashed the cool water on his face to chase the tiredness away.

He quickly changed into fresh clothes and was buttoning his jacket when a soft knock sounded on his door.

Kenning it was Lizzie, he answered curious as to what she wanted. Mayhap something had happened.

"Miss?"

"My lord—Malcolm," she corrected. Her eyes roamed the length of him, a smile lifting the corners of her mouth. "I am glad to see that ye took my advice and sought your bed instead of the hard floor of the hallway."

If that was what she believed, he wouldn't correct her. "Aye."

"I told ye we would still be here in the morn," she laughed softly. "Would ye like to escort us to break our fast in the dining hall?" she asked.

"Indeed. I wouldna have ye dining alone now, would I?"

"I would imagine no'."

Mary exited the room and with the two women looped arm in arm, they made their way downstairs. Once in the dining hall, Mary excused herself to sit off to the side. Malcolm would have had no concerns with the maid joining them, but he understood her reluctance to do so. Even though the two of them seemed to be friends, the maid still kenned her station and would do naught to draw attention to her or Lizzie by acting as if she were more.

Lizzie accepted a cup of tea from the serving maid, and he asked for a newspaper and a cup of the Turkish coffee that the innkeeper had mentioned previously. It was supposedly strong in flavor, and Malcolm looked forward to trying it hoping that it was true. He needed to be at full attention on the next leg of their journey.

A frown marred Lizzie's pretty face as she looked him in the eye.

"'Tis something the matter, Lass?"

"Aye. It appears that e'en though ye finally went to bed, ye didna get as much sleep as ye needed, Sir."

"Malcolm," he reminded her gently, not bothering to correct her about why he was tired. He would let her believe he didn't stand watch for the rest of the night after they'd parted.

"Sir," she insisted. "There are many around that would expect such formalities being used. That aside, your eyes look tired. I feel sad that I am the cause."

"Miss," he said, taking her earlier statement into consideration. "I appreciate your concern. 'Tis no fault of yours, I assure ye."

She said nothing further as she broke her fast on poached eggs, scones, and clotted cream.

"How long will we be traveling today? Yesterday was quite the long stint and I will admit it was quite tiresome. E'en if I did have trouble sleeping," she added.

Guilt pierced his gut. That was not his intention when he'd set their journey. "I will take that into consideration."

"Please do," she said with a tinge of haughtiness to her voice.

He leaned forward and dropped his voice so that only she could hear him. "I would watch your demeanor, Miss. Need I remind ye of your current situation?" He didn't wait for her to answer. "Finish breaking your fast. We leave shortly."

Eyes round in surprise at his shift in attitude, she snapped her mouth shut. But then she pushed from the table. "I fear I have eaten my fill. I shall ready myself for the journey.

That same pinch of guilt resurfaced, but he ignored it. The lass needed to remember the seriousness of the crimes of which she was being investigated for.

Just as he needed to stay focused on his job and unveiling the truth. That was all he needed to do. Once they were in Stonehaven and her guilt or innocence had been proven, he would leave her behind in the hands of the necessary handlers.

And he could erase her from his memory.

But as he sipped his coffee, he kenned he was lying to himself. He snapped open the paper and whistled low. Overnight, the Phantom Prowler had struck again. At an estate near the center of town.

He'd been sleeping outside of Lizzie's door. Could she have possibly managed to sneak out of the room without his knowledge?

IN THE CARRIAGE, Lizzie sat beside Mary as the hours seemed to tick by slowly. She was attempting to read a book to no avail. She would read a page and when it was time to turn to the next, she realized she couldn't remember anything she'd just read.

Currently, she'd been reading the same page for the fifth time.

Malcolm consumed her mind. The man was frustrating. Hot and cold. Sweet and sour. Caring and gruff.

As he stated earlier this morn, she was well aware that she was his prisoner. Whatever quiet time they had shared the night before evaporated with the darkness. The light shining anew on her predicament.

He still thought she was a thief, maddening as that was. She was certain no matter how many times she explained, the only way he would ever believe her was when they arrived at Tolton Hall and he saw the picture of her grandmama.

Then, and only then, would it be clear.

She sighed and closed the book on her lap. "Can we stop soon, please? I need to stretch my legs."

Malcolm assessed her with a raised brow. No doubt trying to figure out if she was making excuses.

"I also need to attend to personal matters, mind ye." She didn't, but if he was looking for excuses, there was one. Surely, he wouldn't deny her the stop when such things were needed to be tended to.

He knocked sharply on the carriage wall and she heard the footman call out to the horses as they began to slow.

Space was what was needed. Space from Malcolm so she could think clearly.

His presence soaked up the entirety of the carriage. So much so it was as if she were suffocating on his scent.

Even if it was a most pleasing scent.

Since their conversation in the dining hall at the inn, it was like he'd erected an invisible barrier around himself to keep her at a distance.

The carriage halted, rocking them back and forth and when the door swung open, Malcolm stepped out.

Poking his head back in, he addressed them. "Both of ye stay put whilst I check the surrounding area. I will let ye ken if 'tis safe to wander."

"Where do ye think we are," Mary asked after Malcolm had shut the door.

Lizzie shrugged. "I've no' any idea." She glanced out the window and could see naught but trees on either side. "It looks as if we are in the middle of the forest."

"Do ye think we are safe? There could be reivers about."

"The earl willna let us out of his sight if it isna. Whether he likes it or no', we are his responsibility. 'Tis his duty to ensure our safety."

Mary frowned. "What do ye mean by that, Miss?"

"We are in his care for this journey, Mary. If any harm came to us, he would have my parents to answer to. Papa wouldna take kindly to that."

"That part is understood, Miss. Why do ye say whether he likes it or no'? As if he had no choice and if he did, he would choose differently."

Mary hadn't seen or heard the conversation she'd shared with Malcolm earlier. When Lizzie thought back on it, she tried to assess where exactly it went wrong. Mayhap it was her questions about whether or not he was married.

They seemed to touch a sensitive spot, though she didn't ken why. Mayhap he lost a wife that he loved dearly. She kenned better not to pry. Her mama always told her that her inquisitive manner would get her into trouble.

The door opened and Malcolm stuck his head in.

"All is clear, ladies. Stay together and stay close. I will remain at the edge of the woods. If anything spooks ye, call out."

His voice was clipped as he spoke and he didn't meet her gaze when he offered her his hand to step out.

"Dinna tarry. Make haste and we will be back on our way."

Lizzie remained silent as she stepped past him, Mary at her side. Looking over her shoulder she saw Malcolm following them. True to his word, he stopped at the edge of the trees as they entered thick brush.

"I dinna care for this, Miss."

"'Tis fine, Mary. We are just walking and stretching our legs. Ye must admit after being cramped into the carriage for the past two days the freedom feels nice."

"Verra true, but let us no' venture too deep."

"Och, Mary, ye fash for naught. But we willna go far." She turned toward the spot they'd entered in the woods, and she could just barely see the outline of the earl as he, true to his word, stood guard.

After a few more minutes of walking, they stopped to relieve themselves. Above them, the leaves which had started to turn color, rustled around them.

"Shall we make our way back, Miss? We dinna want to keep the earl waiting."

Lizzie sighed. Of course, Mary was right, but she wished to stay in the trees just a little longer.

"Let us sit for a moment."

Mary shifted on her feet, her eyes trailing to where Malcolm would be waiting. "Miss…"

Patting the ground beside where she sat, Lizzie waited for Mary to join her. "The longer ye stand there indecisive, the longer we will be here. Sit. 'Twill be fine."

Finally, her maid settled next to her.

Lizzie wrapped her arms around her knees, resting her chin atop them. "Isna it beautiful, Mary? 'Tis so silent and peaceful here. No sounds of carriage wheels, or horses, or people calling out to one another. Just the trees swaying to and fro. The birds tweeting to each other. 'Tis most lovely."

Mary, who remained silent beside her, just nodded as she looked warily toward Malcolm.

The minutes passed and she wondered if Malcolm was growing restless. Would he think they ran? It would be stupid of them to do so. She had no idea where they were. Running would surely lead to death. Either from exposure or to whatever or whomever they might cross in these woods.

And Malcolm still held her grandmama's earrings. Still, she enjoyed the serenity.

Until a very angry Malcolm appeared before them making her yelp in surprise. Damn him. How was he so silent? She swore his boots mustn't actually touch the ground. That was the only explanation for him to make his way through the woods without a sound.

"'Tis time we continue," he said gruffly. "Have ye had time to..." He waved his hand in the air instead of finishing the question.

Mary jumped to her feet. "Aye, my lord. We were just on our way back." She dipped into a curtsy and then tugged on Lizzie's hand.

He narrowed his eyes on her as she still sat stubbornly on the ground.

"It doesna appear that ye were about to return."

"We were, my lord. Miss Lizzie gets so tired sometimes, she just needs to sit and rest for a bit. She's rested now. Are ye no', miss?"

Bless Mary. Her attempt at excusing Lizzie's behavior was appreciated. But her maid didn't need to fib on her account.

Lizzie stood, brushing the twigs and fallen leaves from her gown. "Aye, Mary. We were just returning." She pushed past Malcolm, kenning that the move was entirely improper, but trudged forward anyway.

"Lizzie," his low voice called from behind her and she cursed herself as she stopped.

Mary stopped as well.

"Ye can go on to the carriage, Mary. We willna be far behind."

Her eyes darted from Malcolm to Lizzie, and back again, unsure of what to do.

Lizzie smiled reassuringly. "'Tis fine, Mary. We will be along shortly."

The maid nodded and headed back to the road.

"Why were ye sitting in the woods? Were ye hoping I would forget about ye and leave?"

She huffed. "Nay. Why would I do that?"

"To get away," he answered.

"Sir, that would be the most absurd idea. If I had thought it," she added. "Surely, ye think I am daft if that is what ye thought I was doing. Ye have my grandmama's jewelry and ye ken where I live. 'Twould be most stupid of me to attempt an escape when ye would just find me anyway." She crossed her arms in front of her chest. "Besides, I've naught to run from. As I've stated before, I am no' a thief and that jewelry is mine. Now that I've found it, I willna leave it."

His eyes darkened like storm clouds on a rainy night. "Let us get back to the carriage and continue this godforsaken journey. Ye are trying my patience, Lass," he warned.

A warning she completely ignored. "Might I remind ye, this journey is being done at your insistence?"

"Nay, ye dinna," he huffed. "But if ye canna follow orders, I will ensure that ye do."

Orders? She stomped her foot on the ground, kenning she was acting like a petulant child. "Daresay, what do ye propose to do? If any harm comes to me, ye will have to answer to my papa. And he willna take kindly to his daughter being hurt."

He grabbed her elbow and started pulling her forward, back to the road.

"I didna say I would harm ye, Lass. Nor would I. I dinna hurt ladies. But I will do what must be done if ye dinna listen."

"And I am no' some soldier ye can order about." She dug her heels in the ground, but he was so strong it did naught more than irritate him.

He spun to her. "Ye most definitely are'na. Soldiers listen to orders, they doona disregard them."

In one swift move, he bent and threw her over his shoulder like a heathen.

CHAPTER NINE

"**P**UT ME DOWN," she yelled, peppering his back with her fists and kicking her legs.

Malcolm had the urge to swat her arse to get her to stop but held his anger in check.

He was a bit embarrassed at his actions. The lass was pushing all his buttons. He had agreed to let her stretch her legs and tend to nature's call, but hell's teeth. She had been in the woods for far longer than necessary.

Not kenning if something had happened to her and her maid, after some time, he decided to go in to track them down. Only to hear her maid urging her to go back, and for the lass to refuse and delay.

And her mouth. It was sharp as a tack. She tested his very limits and once he'd had enough, without thought, he picked her up and threw her over his shoulder and headed back toward the road, ignoring her pleas to set her back down.

He would not.

Not until they were at the carriage and he was stuffing her inside.

"Your actions are'na that of an earl. I thought ye were supposed to be chivalrous?"

Now she was trying to belittle him? He grunted. The lass had some nerve. He would not show her the satisfaction of seeing that her words were getting to him. Nay, he would not let her bother him.

They burst through the woods. His coachman's eyes widened at the sight of the lass on his shoulders, but he remained silent as he held the door open.

Pushing her inside, she sat down with a huff next to her maid, and he followed her in, taking a seat across from her.

"Ye, Sir, are a barbarian," she spat.

He leveled her with a glare. "I suggest ye watch your sharp tongue, Lass. Lest ye forget to whom ye are speaking."

She crossed her arms like a spoilt tot and gazed out the window.

It was where her eyes remained as they bounced along the bumpy road. The skies darkened and soon, the pitter-patter of rain sounded on the roof above them.

Damn it. He could only hope that the rain wasn't accompanied by thunder and lightning. Because no matter how irked he was with the lass's actions, if he witnessed the scene that unfolded before him previously, he kenned that he would not be able to resist comforting her. No matter how aggravating she may be.

The carriage jerked to a violent halt and lurched to the right. The coachman yelled something he couldn't quite hear. The carriage rocked back and forth but didn't seem to be moving.

Hell, what now?

He pierced the women with a pointed stare. "Stay right here." Then exited the coach and slammed the door behind him.

Looking at the back of the carriage, he whistled. A huge rut held the right wheel, which had splintered into several pieces.

"Shite!" He pushed his hands through his dampening hair as the rain continued to fall. The rain must have washed out part of the road causing the rut. "Did ye no' see the hole?" He asked the man that was nervously walking around the carriage.

"Nay, my lord. I didna."

Malcolm sighed. "We canna do anything about it now. We will have to lift the carriage out of the rut and change the wheel."

His coachman shook his head. "I doona have a spare wheel, my lord. We can lift the carriage, but I will have to go find a new wheel."

He bit his tongue at the knowledge that they were to be stranded here for who kenned how long. And at the fact that they were traveling without a wheel in case something like this very thing happened.

"Mayhap we can repair it once we see the damage." But even as he said the words, he could see that repairs were not possible.

He went around the side and opened the door. "Out," he commanded.

"In the rain?" Lizzie asked in disbelief.

"Lass, ye are trying my last nerve. We need to move the carriage out from where 'tis stuck. 'Twill be easier to do if ye two arena in it. Safer as well," he added to lessen the sting.

"Come, Mary. Let us seek cover under the trees whilst the men work on the carriage." Lizzie made her way around them and moved to the side of the road.

"Dinna stray too far," he warned.

Lizzie rolled her eyes but for once did as she was told and stopped at the tree line and watched them work.

The wheel was stuck something fierce and it wasn't just a matter of lifting the carriage out of the rut.

Malcolm studied the hole. Intuition telling him that something was amiss.

"Does this look natural to ye, John?" he asked the coachman.

The man shook his head as he tried to dig the wheel out of the mud. He sat back on his heels, assessing the area. "Nay, my lord. The hole is too perfect to be done by Mother Nature. 'Tis the perfect width to snag an unsuspecting wheel. The narrowness also makes it hard to detect until upon it."

Malcolm stood and scanned the trees, his ears listening for any noises that would be too big for an animal.

"Ladies, come forward from the trees." His voice was low. If someone was watching them, he didn't want to give them any inkling that he was aware of them.

"We are fine here, thank ye," Lizzie snapped.

Gritting his teeth, he approached the women. "I need ye closer to the carriage."

"Whye'er for?"

"Are ye always this obstinate?" He shook his head. "Ne'er mind. I dinna want to ken your answer. I want ye to stay close."

Her eyes narrowed and she looked behind her at the woods. "Are we no' safe?" she asked quietly.

"Ye are. I would just prefer if ye were nearby." He didn't want to alarm the women and he said a silent prayer that for just this once, she listened.

With a final look at the trees, she gave him a curt nod, and grasped Mary's hand, pulling her maid toward him.

"Just stay clear of where the carriage might roll if we can loosen it. I dinna want either of ye getting hurt."

He and John went back to work on digging out the wheel. When they finally got it free, they tried to lift the carriage, but its weight was too much.

"I dinna think we will be able to get it out, my lord," John muttered after several attempts.

Malcolm swiped his forearm across his brow. His man was right. They would need to enlist help. He moved to the back of the carriage and rummaged through his bag, his fingers closing around his pistol. With his back to the women, he maneuvered his holster on and slipped the pistol inside. He didn't want to frighten them, but he would be damned if he let them be vulnerable in this situation.

"Take one of the horses and ride to the closest town. Secure some men and a new wheel."

"My lord?"

"I will stay with the women to ensure their safety."

John bowed. "Aye, my lord. I shall return swiftly."

Malcolm nodded, but he doubted it. They were hours away from anyone that would be of help for what they needed. John may come across some men to enlist for what they needed, but the wheel would be another story.

He watched as John climbed one of the horses and trotted down the road.

"The coachman is leaving us?" Lizzie asked.

"One of us had to go and recruit help and I wasna about to leave ye two alone." His eyes went to the woods again. The hairs on the back of his neck stood up. He kenned someone was watching them. The question was, were they there to help or harm?

LIZZIE COULDN'T HELP the shiver that overtook her body. Something wasn't right. Malcolm looked far too serious as he gazed at the trees.

"Are ye certain we are safe?" she whispered, searching the trees but seeing naught.

"Aye," he said quietly.

She worried her lower lip between her teeth. All she could see were branches and leaves, thick tree trunks, and then darkness deep within the woods.

"Mayhap we should start walking toward town. It canna be that far?" she asked hopefully.

"'Twill be better if we stay here. John will be back soon. He'll bring help and then we'll be on the road before we ken it."

The whole time Malcolm spoke, he didn't look at her. Instead, his eyes were focused on the trees.

"I—"

"Lass, please. I ken what 'tis best. Do ye and Mary have cloaks in your bags?"

"Aye," she confirmed, wondering why he asked.

"Get them and put them on. 'Twill keep the chill off ye. I dinna want ye to come down with an ague."

She didn't appreciate being told what to do, but the serious tone of his voice had her moving to do as he said, instead of being objectionable.

Locating their cloaks, they slipped them over their shoulders. "Should we build a fire?"

"Nay."

"It may get cold. If ye dinna want us to become ill 'tis only proper."

"We dinna want to bring any more attention to ourselves than we already have with our stuck carriage."

The sound of a twig snapping drew Malcolm's attention back to the woods. "Go to the side of the carriage, ladies," he ordered tersely, albeit softly, and that was when she noticed the pistol tucked into his side.

She sucked in a breath and hurried to do as she was told, she and Mary huddled together, watching Malcolm move toward the woods.

A hand sneaked around from behind and covered her mouth.

"Well, what 'ave we here?" an unfamiliar voice whispered near her ear, his foul breath infiltrating her senses.

Without a second thought she clamped down on the hand and stomped on the man's foot. He howled, raising his hand to strike her.

She braced for the hit.

"I suggest ye step away from the lady," Malcolm ordered, his voice cold as ice.

Pistol in hand, it was pointed at the filthy man. He looked and smelled as if he hadn't bathed in ages and she tried to ignore the awful taste lingering in her mouth. He looked at Malcolm, smiling a toothless grin, as he put his hands up.

Mary wrapped her arms around Lizzie, and they huddled together against the carriage.

Why was he smiling? The look on Malcolm's face was terrifying.

Another man, just as dirty as the one standing in front of them, stepped out of the woods and her breath caught.

Was this an ambush? She'd heard about them from her father's travels but had never experienced one before.

"Malcolm!" Lizzie yelled as the man stepped up behind him, his hand raised high, ready to bring down a club upon his head.

With a deft swiftness, Malcolm spun, ducking out of the way of the blow that just missed him. He threw an elbow out, catching the man on the chin, causing him to stumble back. Striking him with the butt of his pistol, the man collapsed in a heap.

Pointing his pistol at the two men, he stalked them like they were his prey. His eyes impossibly dark. His face fierce and set in stone.

The man that grabbed her earlier reached out, but she and Mary stepped back with a shriek. He kept advancing, and a shot pierced through the air, echoing in the silence of the woods. The man clasped his chest, looking down at his hand that was covered in blood, his eyes wide in disbelief.

"I warned ye." Malcolm kicked out, his boot landing on the man's chest and pushing him into the other man, who lost his balance.

As he tried to scrabble to his feet, Malcolm reached out grabbing him by the shoulders before spinning him about. His fist pounded into the man's meaty jaw. Once. Twice. Three times.

The sound was sickening to Lizzie's ears.

The man went limp and Malcolm looked around wildly. He holstered his pistol and ran up to them.

"Are ye alright, Lass?" His hands rubbed up and down her arms as he assessed her.

She nodded, unable to speak. He'd saved her. Saved Mary. Saved them both.

Against two men. By himself.

"Get in the carriage, ladies." He pushed his hands through his hair as he looked at the two men on the ground.

She was certain he'd killed one of them.

"I need to secure these louses afore they wake." He opened the door to the carriage and ushered them inside. "I shan't be long. Stay put. Please."

When he didn't budge, she nodded her head, and then he was gone. She heard him rummaging through their bags, and the tearing of material.

"Did ye see how fierce the earl was, Miss? He saved ye from the reivers."

"Us, Mary. He saved the both of us. I've no doubt he would have acted the same whether I was here or no'."

They watched out the window of the carriage as he bound their hands and legs then secured them each to a tree.

"Are ye certain ye both are well," Malcolm asked again as he stepped inside the carriage.

"Aye. Thank ye, my lord."

He was opening and closing the fingers of his right hand, the knuckles bruised and starting to swell.

She moved in front of him, taking his hand in hers. "Ye're hurt."

"Nay, Lass. I am fine."

But he winced when she touched one of his knuckles that had a deep cut on it. Without a thought, she lifted her gown and managed to rip some cloth from her chemise. She dabbed at the wound and he let out a low hiss.

"Ye acted so verra bravely."

"Any man would," he countered, his eyes boring into hers.

It was as if they were the only two people in the carriage. Mary melted away. The men outside melted away. It was only the two of them there in this moment.

"I dinna think any man would have done what ye just did. Ye fought with two men. And won."

He brought his other hand up and stroked her jaw.

She leaned into the caress.

"I couldna let aught happen to ye, Lass."

Her breath hitched at his words. Words that sounded almost like a confession. His eyes flared as they focused on her mouth. Her hands stilled and she swallowed.

Hard.

Did he want to kiss her?

CHAPTER TEN

L IZZIE'S PINK TONGUE darted out and wet her lips and he had to
hold back the groan that had naught to do with his sore knuckles
and everything to do with how he wanted to wrap her in his arms and
capture her mouth in his.

The feeling he'd had when she called out as he scanned the woods
earlier was one he did not want to experience ever again. The cretin
that was aiming to strike Lizzie might live, but he didn't deserve to.

Not after what he'd done.

He couldn't stop stroking her cheek. The way she leaned into his
fingers and closed her eyes had his cock stirring to life.

Dropping his hand he tamped his lust and pulled his other hand
from her grasp.

"'Tis fine, Lass. 'Tis just a bruise. I've suffered much worse."

Her brows furrowed at that, but she gave him a quick nod, and
went back and settled beside Mary.

"What do we do now?"

His intuition had been right that something was amiss.

Both of the men were tied securely, and even when they woke up,
they wouldn't be able to free themselves. Once John returned with
help, he would send the men back to alert the authorities.

It was just a matter of how long that would be. Mayhap he would
get lucky and come across a well-stocked village that had an extra
wheel to spare along with a few men. That would be the best scenario.

"Now we wait. We canna go anywhere with the carriage in its

current state."

"Do ye think there will be others?" she asked quietly.

She didn't have to explain who she meant. She was worried that other men with ill intentions would try to attack them.

"Nay. Men like them dinna usually share the areas they control. I am certain we are safe."

"What if they awaken? They will attack again, aye?"

He shook his head. "They are'na getting out of the ties that bind them to those trees. They will still be there when authorities come to collect them later."

She nodded and clasped her hands in her lap.

Not kenning what else to say, he remained silent as he watched her. Mary wrapped her arms around Lizzie's shoulders and the lass collapsed into them, a soft sob falling from her lips, piercing his heart.

He was telling the truth about them being safe.

But seeing how frightened she'd been tugged at him. Made him want to kiss all her worries away. Promise her that he would always protect her.

All the while, that little voice niggled in his head. Reminding him she was a thief. He was just doing a job.

Minutes ticked by, then hours, until finally they heard the sounds of hooves pounding on the road outside the carriage.

Lizzie sat up, her back rigid, eyes round in fear.

"Shhhh." He held his finger to his lips.

A familiar whistle sounded, and he smiled. "'Tis John. Let us hope he brings help." He patted her on the leg. "Stay put for now."

Outside, on the road, John approached, followed by four burly men.

"My lord. As instructed, I've brought reinforcements." The men dismounted, and a grunt from the trees had them shifting their sights to the woods.

"My lord? What has happened?"

"We were attacked. The ladies are fine," he quickly added as John's face grew dark with concern. "When ye return to town, ye will need to alert your authorities," he said to the men there to help.

Two hours later, the carriage bounced along the rocky road, good as new. The men John had found were all farmers, used to tilling the land, hence their strength. They had made quick work of lifting the carriage out of the ditch and assisting with getting the wheel changed.

Before they left to return home, they gathered the attackers, securing them to their horses to bring them to town to face their punishment.

John explained the town was quite nice. The people kind. There was an inn that they could rest for the night. It wasn't where they had originally planned to stop, but this delay had put them way behind schedule.

The women were quiet as they rode along. He thought Lizzie may have fallen asleep until he caught her eyes watching him.

Something had changed between them. He couldn't explain it.

The carriage slowed before rocking to a halt and John swung open the door, announcing their arrival.

He looked out the door. They were stopped in front of a white-washed stone building. Atop the door, a wrought iron sign with the letters INN swung to and fro in the wind.

Inside, Lizzie and Mary hung back as he spoke with the innkeeper, who, unfortunately, informed them he had only one room available.

Gazing out the window at the dark sky, he nodded, accepting the key. It was too late to push on, and the women had been through enough for one day.

And the horses needed rest.

Up the stairs, he pushed open the door, waiting for Lizzie and Mary to walk through before following them inside.

Lizzie cocked her head to the side, confused.

"There is only one room available."

She opened her mouth to speak, but he held his hand up.

"Dinna fash. I will sleep in the hall, 'tis no' an issue. But I would like to clean up first. After ye both have had the chance to do so, of course."

"Of course, my lord."

"I'll have hot water brought up. I'll return after ye've had time to tend to your needs."

With a bow, he backed out of the room, leaning on the door after he closed it. Thoughts of the lass bathing flooded his mind and he pushed off the door. Shaking his head to rid it of his errant thoughts.

As he tracked down a maid to request a tub of water, he still couldn't rid his mind of the images running rampant through his head.

LIZZIE GROANED AS she eased into the tub of hot water. The day had been filled with stress and as she soaked she felt her limbs loosen.

They'd been so taut. But that was no surprise considering all that had happened.

"How much longer do ye think we have until we arrive in Stonehaven?" she asked Mary as she passed Lizzie a soapy washcloth.

"I've no idea, Miss. I am certain Lord Kennedy can tell ye."

"I fear he finds me naught but trouble, Mary. First, he thinks me a thief, then he has to save me from an actual thief."

Mary giggled. "Och, I am no' so sure he minds."

Water sloshed over the edge as she sat up abruptly. "Whate'er do ye mean?"

Mary shrugged. "'Tis no' my place to say, miss."

"'Tis when I ask ye, Mary."

She plucked the cloth from Lizzie's hand and began to wash her back. "There is something about the way he looks at ye. I dinna think he truly believes ye are the prowler."

Resting her hands on the sides of the tub, she rolled her head from side to side to ease some of the tightness there as Mary washed her back. "Mayhap no'. But I believe he still sees me as a nuisance."

"Ye fash overmuch. He didna have to go to all this trouble to prove ye are'na the thief. There were other ways for him to do so. Nay, I think deep down he's enjoying the time spent with ye."

Lizzie scoffed as she leaned back in the tub. "He has a funny way of showing it." She bit her lip and thought about the coming night. "I canna have him sleeping in the hall tonight. "'Tis bad enough he did last night when I was unawares. But now that I ken? I refuse to allow the earl to sleep on the floor in the hallway."

"What do ye propose, then, miss?"

"He will have to sleep in here." She nodded her head, mind made up.

"Miss?"

"I ken this trip has been unorthodox, but so far I have managed to ensure piety. I dinna ken how easy that will be if we share a room. 'Twould be most improper."

"On the contrary, I think he believes he hasna ensured propriety. That 'twould be putting your honor and reputation in question. He doesna seem the type of man to do that."

Mary held out a towel and Lizzie stepped out of the tub and wrapped herself in its warmth. "Mayhap ye are right. I dinna ken what to think anymore. He confuses me. One minute he's kind and caring, and the next he's cool and dismissive."

A knock at the door made her jump.

"Ladies?" Malcolm called from the other side. "May I enter?"

"Nay!" they both called out at the same time.

"Um, verra well. I shall return in a bit."

"Come on, Miss. Let us get ye dressed before he returns," Mary giggled. "We mustn't make him wait twice. He is an earl after all."

"Fine. But dinna forget, earl or no', he is still my captor."

Mary harrumphed as she laid a dress out on the bed. "Ye canna lie, miss. If he is your captor, then I am the queen."

"Shush, Mary. Do ye think we would be on this journey on our own?"

"Nay." She held up the dress for Lizzie to step into. "Howe'er, we would still be on our way back to Stonehaven, one way or another."

Lizzie rolled her eyes. "Why must ye always make sense?"

"Sit, and I'll brush out your hair." She pointed to the chair and Lizzie obeyed. "'Tis a tangled mess after the trials of the day."

Lizzie watched Mary through the reflection of the looking glass as she brushed then braided her hair before finally twisting it onto a knot at her nape.

She handed her maid pins one by one as she secured the bun, ensuring it would stay in place.

"There, ye are all set."

"What of ye?"

"Och, dinna fash about me. When ye and Lord Kennedy go down to sup, I will go with the other servants and clean up then."

She felt a bit guilty that Mary couldn't enjoy the same comforts she did.

But before she could think on it any longer, Malcolm knocked asking for entry.

His huge frame seemed to take up all the space in the room as he stood there. For a moment he said naught. Just looked at her as if he wanted to devour her and she couldn't help the shiver that crept up her spine.

He cleared his throat and looked away.

"Ye look lovely, Lass."

She curtsied in thanks. She grabbed Mary's hand. "We will go downstairs and await ye there."

"I shan't be long."

Nodding, she didn't say a word as they left the room and Mary closed the door shut behind them.

"That look was pure lust if I've e'er seen it," Mary whispered.

"Hush, Mary! Dinna say such things," Lizzie snapped. But inside, deep inside her belly, was a warm sensation she couldn't ignore.

It only happened when the earl was near. Her skin heated as if it were on fire and her stomach knotted. She wasn't sure she'd be able to eat when Malcolm finished washing up.

Hopefully her stomach had time to calm before he joined them. As they waited, they sat and sipped tea.

A lass, appearing to be about Lizzie's age, smiled and waved her over. Not wanting to be rude, Lizzie picked up her tea and saucer and walked over.

"I'm Rosalie. Ye look a wee bit lonely and thought I'd offer companionship. Are ye waiting for someone?" She pointed to the chair across from her. "Please, sit."

Lizzie slipped into the chair. "Lizzie. 'Tis a pleasure to make your acquaintance."

Mary stayed behind standing near the wall.

"Is she your attendant?" Rosalie asked, dipping her head to Mary.

"Aye."

"She can join mine to sup. She's with the other's near the kitchen."

Mary gave a curtsy. "Aye, miss. I shall do that. If ye need anything, please call for me."

Lizzie watched her walk out of the room and disappear down the hall.

"Where are ye traveling from?" Rosalie asked, her eyes darting toward the door.

"Stonehaven. I'm returning home from a brief trip to Twynholm."

"Is that so? How did ye like it?"

"Pardon?"

"Twynholm. Did ye enjoy it?"

"Oh, well, I wasna there verra long. I just attended a party of a family friend."

Lizzie couldn't explain why, but the woman made her uneasy. The conversation, whilst could be considered small talk, seemed a bit intrusive.

"I am making my way back to Edinburgh."

"That's nice," Lizzie said, unsure of what she was supposed to say.

She wished Malcolm would hurry up and save her from whatever this was.

Her prayers were answered when a few moments later, cleaned up from their travels, dressed in clean breeches, shiny black boots, a white linen shirt, and black waistcoat, Malcolm entered through the door. His eyes searching the room, until they landed on her and he smiled.

His honey hair was still damp, and even though it was short, it had a slight wave to it.

"Well, what have we here?" Rosalie commented as she watched Malcolm approach, licking her lips.

Lizzie looked at her at first mortified, but that was quickly replaced with fast rising anger. Or was it jealousy?

What did she have to be jealous about? Her captor catching the attention of a stranger?

"Ladies," Malcolm drawled as he approached.

"Hello, Sir," Rosalie drawled as she held her hand out.

Malcolm dipped and kissed it, and Lizzie scoffed, rolling her eyes.

He had never kissed her hand in greeting. Granted, she had never offered, but that was beside the point.

"Miss Barclay," Malcolm addressed her, remembering their previous conversation about putting up the correct front in public. "Are ye ready to eat?"

Rosalie cleared her throat. "I believe introductions are in order, are they no'?"

Lizzie bit the inside of her cheek to stop her from saying something snide that she would regret. She took a deep breath and smiled.

"Of course, where are my manners? Lord Kennedy, this is Rosalie. I apologize, I didna get your last name."

Rosalie waved her hand in the air, dismissing Lizzie's inquiry. "Lord Kennedy? Well, 'tis a pleasure to meet ye, sir." She stood and dipped into a curtsy, pushing forward so that her breasts drew attention.

Or at least that was her attempt. Instead, Malcolm cleared his throat and offered his hand to Lizzie. "I fear I am famished after our travels today. I am certain ye are as well."

She nodded and stood, letting him pull her away from the table.

Rosalie sputtered, and Lizzie was pretty sure she would have stomped her foot on the ground if she wouldn't look like a child having a tantrum.

Malcolm bent to her. "What was that all about?" he asked near her ear, his breath fanning her face.

Lizzie shrugged. "I honestly canna say. That was truly the oddest conversation I have e'er had."

He pulled out a chair for her and she took a seat.

He settled across from her, unfolding the napkin and placing it on his lap. "Where is Mary?"

"She's with the other servants, washing up and supping."

Nodding, he looked over at the table where Rosalie had sat back down. She was currently shooting them a glare that Lizzie did not understand.

"I dinna ken what is wrong with her." His brow wrinkled. "What was her name?"

"Rosalie."

"Aye, I dinna ken what her issue is."

"I think that is clear. Look at the way she keeps looking over here."

He grunted in disinterest.

And a little spark of hope ignited in her chest.

"She is looking in the wrong place for whatever she is searching for." He asked for a whisky from a passing server. "I've no need to look anywhere else."

CHAPTER ELEVEN

MALCOLM WANTED TO kick himself. Had he actually just said that? Hell's teeth, he was getting soft.

No matter how Rosalie looked at him, she had no effect on him. Truth be told, she looked like she could work in one of the local whorehouses. She probably did. He had no idea what she'd told Lizzie, but he was certain whatever it was, was a lie.

He was surprised the innkeeper allowed her to sully his patronage. It was a surefire way to ensure he would never return, especially with a reputable lass such as Lizzie.

Reputable? He almost laughed. She was a possible thief. That made her no more reputable than Rosalie.

Lizzie had a sour look on her face. "Is something amiss?"

"Nay. 'Tis naught. If ye'd like to sup with Rosalie, ye are welcome to. I am fine dining on my own." Her voice was clipped as she spoke.

"I—" He snapped his mouth shut as he searched for the right words. But what was it that he wanted to say? "I dinna wish that. I am quite comfortable with my current company."

Her cheeks flushed in the most adorable way, and once again, he had to remind himself that this wasn't some courtship he was doing. It was a job.

It seemed to take forever for the food to be served. When it finally was, they ate in awkward silence, stealing glances.

He was too old for this shite. He wasn't some schoolboy seeing his first pretty girl.

He was a grown man for Christ's sake.

"I canna eat another bite," Lizzie announced, dabbing at the corners of her mouth before setting her napkin on her plate.

Mary appeared out of nowhere. "Are ye ready to retire, miss?"

"Aye." She stood and turned to him and dropped into a curtsy. "Thank ye for the company during dinner, my lord."

He stood and nodded. "I will be up shortly."

He watched her walk out of the room, his eyes never leaving her arse.

"Another whisky," he called to the server as she passed, waving his glass.

She returned with a bottle and went to pour him a glass.

"Just leave the bottle. Ye can add it to my bill."

As he drank, his eyes remained where Lizzie had disappeared. What the hell was he going to do for the night?

One room.

One damn room.

He sucked down two more glasses of whisky and pushed back from the table. He needed to make sure the women were safely in their room.

As he left the dining room, an arm snaked around his neck. A mouth close to his ear spoke seductively. "I didna think ye were e'er going to leave the room."

He extricated himself from Rosalie and took a step back. "Sorry, I am no' interested."

She tugged at his lapels, trying to pull him closer, but his feet were planted.

"Come on, now. We can have a great time before ye return to your lady."

"She's no' my lady."

Rosalie smiled wide. "E'en better."

"Nay." He grasped her hands and pulled them off his jacket. "I said

I wasna interested. Ye would do well to heed my words." He pushed past her and took the stairs two at a time.

Fighting the urge to burst through the door, he paused, and took a deep breath before knocking sharply on the door. "'Tis I," he called and waited for an invitation in.

He said it was only so that he could verify their safety. That's what he kept telling himself. But he was also hoping for a glimpse of Lizzie in her nightclothes. He'd had a taste of it the night previously, but he longed for more.

Mary swung the door open and held it wide for him to walk through.

Lizzie was in her nightdress, covered with a robe cinched tight around her small waist.

He bit his lip. He wanted to reach out and tug on the bow and let it fall to the floor.

"I have been thinking and I dinna feel comfortable with ye sleeping on the floor of the hall. 'Tis no' right. Ye are an earl. Ye should be sleeping in the verra best conditions." She paused, smoothing her robe with the palms of her hands. "While I canna offer ye that, we do have only one bed after all. Ye should at least sleep in here."

He closed his eyes. The thought of sleeping in the same room with Lizzie and not being able to touch her sounded like a torture he didn't want to experience.

"'Tis verra kind of ye, Lass. But I dinna think that is wise."

"Is it because ye would rather sleep in Rosalie's bedroom?"

"Miss!" Mary scolded.

Lizzie tilted her chin up stubbornly. "Ye can go then. I am no' holding ye here. Ye've no duty to me. I ken men have," she paused, rolling her lips inward, "needs," she finished quietly.

Mary gasped at her side.

"I will take my leave. No' because of any preconceived *needs* ye think I may have. But because I respect ye and doona want to say anything uncouth in front of ye. I will be back in the morn to gather ye and continue our journey," he snapped and left the room. It took all his might to not slam the door shut.

The last thing he saw was Lizzie standing with her mouth open in surprise. Good. The lass had gone too far insinuating what she had.

He paced the hall for a bit before going downstairs and procuring another whisky. Then he marched his arse back up the stairs and parked it on the floor in front of Lizzie's door. Hopefully this night she would have a better night than the last and she wouldn't feel the need to chase down a glass of warm milk.

Settling against the door, he let himself relax. He'd slept in much more uncomfortable positions in his lifetime. The night would pass slowly, but it would pass and they would be back on the road in the morn.

Malcolm jerked awake, a loud noise startling him, until he realized the time.

Jumping to his feet, he rubbed the sleep out of his eyes with the heels of his hands.

Rolling his head from side to side trying to get the kinks out, his back screamed from the movement. He very much looked forward to sleeping in a bed, though that wouldn't happen until they reached Stonehaven.

Downstairs, the inn was coming to life. Maids were moving about and the kitchen staff were hard at work. The smell of fresh baking bread wafting up and infiltrating his senses. His stomach growled, but he ignored it.

They really needed to get on the road as soon as possible this morn. The events of the day before had put them behind schedule. He pushed off the door and went in search of the innkeeper. There would be no time to break their fast in the dining room today. Instead, he would pay the innkeeper to have his cook prepare them a basket to take on their way.

"Ah, good morn, my lord. I hope the room was to your satisfaction."

"'Twas, thank ye. Could I trouble ye to prepare us a meal for the road? We must be getting on our way."

"Och, so soon," a voice drawled from behind him. "I was hoping we could get to ken each other better today." Rosalie sidled over to him, and he stiffened.

"Ah, I see ye've met my daughter," the innkeeper said, and Malcolm choked down a snarky reply.

Damn. That was unexpected.

"We met last eve, Papa."

"Well, I hope ye werena any trouble. Run along and ask Cook to put something together so that the earl and his wards can break their fast as they travel."

Irritation reddened her face, but she spun and left toward the kitchen. Malcolm had a feeling she didn't like being ordered about. He also had the feeling her father had no idea his daughter was soliciting his guests.

Nodding his thanks, he went upstairs to gather the women. He had enough problems of his own without adding a lonely lass to the equation.

He rapped his knuckles on the door and waited.

Mary answered. "Good morn, my lord."

"'Twill be once we are on the road," he said gruffly.

"I FEAR THE earl is upset with me, Mary. Rightly so, I suppose."

Lizzie had hardly slept all night. She just tossed and turned, kicking herself for the things she had said to Malcolm. It wasn't her place and she should have just kept her mouth shut.

Her mama had oft told her it would get her into trouble one day. It appeared the day had come.

"I am certain he is only grumpy due to having to sleep on the floor again," Mary offered, trying to make her feel better.

It didn't help. She would apologize to Malcolm when they were on the road. Which would be soon, since he was here to gather them up.

His brows were furrowed as he entered the room and gave her a curt nod. His appearance seemed to suck all of the air out of the room.

She and Mary had been up since before dawn. All the tossing and turning she'd done had kept Mary awake, which she felt very bad about. She'd apologized multiple times, but Mary just swept her hand in dismissal. Tired of waiting for sleep to come, she gave up the fight and they both got out of bed and started getting ready for the day.

Because of their delays yesterday, she had an inkling Malcolm would want to be on the road as early as possible this morn, and she wasn't wrong.

He picked up their bags. "Are these all ye have?" he asked gruffly.

"Aye."

Without another word, he walked stiffly out of the room, his mouth in a thin line. They had no choice but to hurry after him. Divine smells from the kitchen wafted through the halls, assaulting her senses and her stomach growled in response. If Malcolm heard, he paid no attention and walked out the door into the cool morning air.

John was waiting for them to exit, stepping forward to take the bags from Malcolm and securing them to the back of the carriage.

Mary followed her inside and they settled on the bench, waiting for Malcolm to join them.

He poked his head inside. "I need to settle up with the innkeeper. I will be back shortly." He backed out, but then stuck his head inside once again. "Dinna go anywhere."

She wasn't sure where he thought they would go. But she nodded and watched him leave.

When he returned a few moments later, he held a cloth covered basket that he brought inside the carriage.

Lizzie kenned what it was immediately. The same smells from the kitchen now filled the interior and as the carriage rocked to a start, she couldn't stop looking longingly at the basket.

Would it be rude to ask if they could break their fast? She worried her lip as she thought about it.

It would, she decided. But then she remembered she had a more pressing matter to attend first.

"My lord," she called, drawing his eyes from the window to her.

He didn't say anything, just raised a brow in question. His blue eyes questioning as he met her own eyes in response.

"I feel I owe ye an apology. Sometimes I speak without thinking, and I fear I did just that last night. I shouldna have said those things, and I apologize for doing so."

The way he looked at her was disconcerting. Was he trying to ascertain if she spoke the truth? She did indeed. She felt awful about what she'd said. It was why she couldn't sleep last night.

After a long silence, he nodded. "Apology accepted. Though I should do the same. I wasna acting gentlemanly in any way."

Pressing her lips together, she hid her smile behind her hand.

"Well, with that out of the way, let us start the day on a new foot," she offered.

"I believe ye are right, Miss. I had the innkeeper prepare a meal to break our fast on the road. Well, I asked him, and he tasked his daughter, Rosalie, to do it."

Lizzie couldn't stop the chuckle that burst from her lips. "She is the innkeeper's daughter?" She asked with surprise. "I would ne'er have guessed that."

"I, too, was quite surprised when I found out this morn."

He smiled warmly and the gesture transformed his whole face. He was very handsome when he dropped the strict countenance he'd been holding.

NOBODY'S ROGUE

"That's also to say I havena checked the items in the basket, so we may either be pleasantly surprised or expectantly disappointed."

"Either way, 'tis naught to do with ye. Ye canna control her actions."

The scents filling the interior had her believing that they would enjoy whatever items were inside, but she supposed she there was always a possibility that she included something untoward.

They enjoyed a pleasant meal, which, surprisingly, only included edible items. Lizzie was delighted as she broke her fast on an array of scones, fruit tarts, and even a boiled egg as the carriage ambled along. Every once in a while, it would lurch them to the right or left and they were careful not to tip their plates.

There was no tea to be had, but Malcolm did offer her sips from his flagon, which was filled with wine. She imagined that wasn't what it usually held so she appreciated the gesture, even if it was a wee bit early to be drinking wine.

Mary ate in silence beside them, her eyes focused on the trees beyond the window.

"My lord," Lizzie called after swallowing a bite from a deliciously warm scone. "We have traveled all these miles together and yet I feel we ken verra little of each other. I think it a splendid idea to rectify that for the remainder of our journey."

He cocked his head as if contemplating her suggestion, and after a sip of wine, nodded. "Where should we begin? What would ye like to ken?"

This was promising. She thought he might turn her down, but this was promising indeed.

"Ye previously said ye werena married. Multiple times," she added. "Have ye e'er been?" She probably shouldn't have started with such a personal question, but she was genuinely curious as to what made Malcolm Kennedy take such concerns. Aye, he had his temper side, but he'd also shown her he could be gentle and kind. She wanted to ken whom he learned that from.

"Nay. I have ne'er wed."

As handsome as he was and an earl, she found that surprising.

"Have ye?"

She snorted. "Absolutely no'. I believe my parents would like to see me wed, but no one has met my papa's expectations. They are exceedingly high."

"Do ye want to marry?"

"Och, aye. When the time is right. And the right man comes along." She ducked her head as she felt her skin flush. Her parents had always been accommodating when it came to marriage concerns. For that, she was extremely grateful.

"Ye are close with your parents? I've heard ye mention them a few times."

She loved them dearly, though she didn't look forward to her arrival home and them learning of her antics. They would be most unhappy.

"They have been verra kind. I can be trying at times," she admitted.

Beside her, Mary chuckled, before squeezing her lips shut, trying not to outright laugh.

"Ye dinna say," Malcolm said dryly. "I'd have ne'er guessed."

She tilted her head to the side and shrugged her shoulders. "I do try."

"But sometimes 'tis just hard?" The corners of his full mouth lifted.

"Ye are teasing me. I do my best, but ofttimes it gets me into trouble."

"Such as attending a party to steal jewelry."

Her eyes rounded. "I have already told ye that is no' what I was doing. Which ye will soon find to be true."

"Mmhhmm" he murmured.

"But aye, they were unaware that I was going to attend the party of Viscount and Viscountess Wilson. And they will be most unhappy about it when they find out," she added, scrunching up her nose.

"How about siblings? Have ye any?"

Her heart sank at the thought of her brother. "I did, but he passed a few years ago."

"I am verra sorry to hear that. Was he sick?"

She shook her head. "Nay. He fought in the war. He was lost just before it ended."

His brows furrowed and he got a faraway look in his eyes. "War is never a winning affair. There are losers on both sides. The loss of life is the saddest outcome."

She could only bob her head up and down. She missed her younger brother dearly. He was kind and loved his family above all else. When duty called, he jumped at the chance.

When she'd seen him off the day he left, she never imagined it would be the last time she would see him. Or hear his voice.

But she didn't want to think about that. She didn't want to be sad. She usually kept the memories of her brother locked away in the recesses of her mind. If she didn't, she would be filled with sorrow all the time. She didn't want to live her life that way. And neither would he.

"Do ye have any siblings?" She wanted the focus off her and her family. He would find out soon enough how much she and her parents loved each other. And the memories of her brother were all around the house.

"I dinna. My parents passed shortly after my mother gave birth to me."

"I am so sorry." Her heart broke at his loss.

"'Tis fine. I dinna remember them. My childhood was filled with nannies and tutors, preparing me for my position as earl."

She thought of how sad of a life that must have been. She couldn't imagine a childhood without her brother. Without her parents. It would have been lonely to say the least.

"That must have been hard on ye."

He shook his head. "'Twasna really. I didna ken any better. And when it came time for me to leave for the war, I didna have to fash o'er a family I was leaving behind."

That part was true.

"What did ye do in the war?"

Malcolm's gaze moved to the window and his eyes darkened. His face suddenly looked somber as if the unpleasant memories were more than he wished to think about.

Suddenly, she felt bad for asking the question, though her intentions were purely innocent as she was only curious.

"Ye dinna have to answer that, my lord. I'm sure it must have been a trying time."

CHAPTER TWELVE

MALCOLM DIDN'T REALLY want to talk about the war. He'd seen too much. Felt too much. And the sting of betrayal still hit him hard. But since Lizzie had shared so much with him, he felt he had to give her some information. He would just leave all the bad parts out.

"I worked with Wellington. Doing surveillance mostly."

"Wow, that is impressive. He must have held ye in verra high standing to work with him directly." She'd heard her papa speak of the man and always gave him high regards.

"I dinna ken that, but I was verra good at what I did." He leaned forward, resting his forearms on his knees as he locked his eyes on hers. "'Tis why I was at the party. Wilson had hired me to ensure the Phantom Prowler didn't attack."

Her eyes rounded. "Do ye really think I am that prowler? Truly?"

He sat back, assessing her. Did he? He had serious doubts. But he wasn't about to tell her that.

"That still remains to be seen. If ye are, I dinna ken how ye werena apprehended before now. Ye do verra sloppy work."

She threw her hands up in exasperation. "Because I am no' the prowler! That alone should prove it."

He chuckled.

"Dinna laugh at me. I am no'."

"Ye keep repeating that, but I did catch ye with your hands deep in the viscountess's chest of jewels."

"Aye, aye, aye." She waved her hand in the air. "Ye will see. My papa will no' be happy at all to find I've been forced to travel with a stranger. 'Tis a good thing Mary is here with me. Otherwise ye'd be forced to marry me for sullying my reputation."

He barked out a laugh. He couldn't help it. "I am sullying your reputation? My dear lass, I think ye are doing a fine job of tarnishing your reputation all on your own."

She crossed her arms and scowled at him.

"I have done no such thing. My reputation remains intact."

Back and forth their conversation went until they stopped early in the afternoon to stretch their legs and rest the horses.

Malcolm realized that he was enjoying their banter perhaps more than he should be. He'd found the morning pleasant and if it weren't for the actual reason they were on this journey he could almost see it as a journey a couple would partake together.

He pushed a hand through his hair and dug his fingers into his scalp. The women were off tending to nature's call, and he thought of his friends that had recently married. Both Nicholas and Alexander were over the moon in love with their new wives. Finlay, too, though his marriage was more recent and it was expected that he would be lost in love.

Had they felt the same way he was feeling now? Not that he was in love with Lizzie. Nay. Not at all. Infatuated, mayhap. Lusted, definitely.

Even when he kenned that was the last feeling he should have running through his body, but damn, the lass awakened every nerve he had.

The gowns she wore accented the swell of her hips, revealed the swell of her bosom. And her scent? She smelled like wildflowers ye would find deep in the meadows of the highlands.

He bit back a growl at the thoughts running rampant in his mind.

"Will we be continuing on soon?" Lizzie asked from behind him.

Startled, he took a step forward, clearing his throat. "Aye, as soon as John readies the horses."

He expected her to walk away and settle in the carriage, but instead she moved beside him, her hands clasped at her waist.

"'Tis a lovely landscape is it no'?" She didn't wait for him to answer before continuing on. "My brother and I would spend whole days running through the trees. My mama would get so angry when I would rip my skirts by snagging them on the branches as we ran as if the devil himself were chasing us." She laughed at the memory and it was a beautiful sound. Her voice transformed when she reminisced of her childhood.

"I'm verra sorry for the loss of your brother, Lass."

She nodded, a small smile lifting the corners of her mouth. "Thank ye. He was a kind, but misguided soul." She swatted at a bug flying near her head. "Looks like John is ready," she said and headed toward the carriage.

He wanted to ask what Lizzie meant about her brother being misguided, but she quickly changed the subject and was gone in a flash, leaving him no time to do so. Maybe she would open up more as they continued on their journey.

Why did he care? Once they arrived at Tolton Hall and he proved her guilt or innocence, his job was done.

Guilty? He turned her in to the authorities and headed home.

Innocent? He left her with her parents and headed home.

Either outcome had him going back to Culzean. Back to his mundane life. That should make him happy. His return home had been blessedly issue free. Unlike his friend Nicholas, who returned home to find his mother had secured him a marriage. Or Alexander, who returned home to find his brother had gambled away the family estate. And then there was Finlay, who returned to find that he had to marry before his birthday or lose his title.

For that, he was thankful. He'd left Culzean in the hands of his trusted estate solicitor and his loyal and capable staff. He had no doubt he would return home to everything being in the same condition.

And it was. Culzean thrived whilst he was away.

But still. He was bored. Aye he'd distracted himself with several women in the city. They were only too eager to jump in his bed—until he couldn't promise them a future. Once they found that out, they walked out the door never to return.

They didn't matter. When one left, there was another there begging to take her place. And who was he to turn away a wanting lass?

After a time, even that got to be monotonous. The nightly dates to the theater, the opera, the endless balls and parties. He'd grown tired of it all.

He longed for an excitement that they couldn't provide.

At one time his friends mentioned to him that he might look into the Glasgow Police. The idea was tempting. The work they could provide would certainly be interesting. A little more exciting than the various work he'd done for his friends, which almost always consisted of him either finding documents, looking into someone's background, or actually finding someone.

Once in a while, he picked up a job such as what Viscount Wilson hired him for—security of sorts, but usually they amounted to naught.

At least this one would occupy his time for a week or so.

LIZZIE KEPT STEALING glances at Malcolm. He'd been lost in his head deep in thought ever since they'd started back on their travels.

"Pence for your thoughts?" She asked, her curiosity getting the best of her.

Snapping out of whatever had his mind preoccupied, Malcolm raised his brows and sighed. "Apologies, Miss. 'Tis naught I'd like to share."

Well, that was unsuccessful. She didn't ken why she cared so much whether or not he conversed with her. She enjoyed the sound of his voice. The deep timbre she found somehow relaxing. Much more so than the grind of the rocks and gravel beneath the carriage wheels. The jostling of the reins as the horses pulled them forward to their next destination.

"Is the plan to stop at the same inn we were originally supposed to stay last night or to push forward since we will only have a few hours of travel today?"

Malcolm frowned and tilted his head as he assessed her. "I had thought on that and we will stop there tonight. I think some extended time outside of the carriage would do us all good."

She nodded. "Thank ye. 'Tis verra kind of ye."

He winked and her stomach fluttered. Actually fluttered as if butterflies had taken flight within her belly.

"No matter the situation we find ourselves in, I do care about your well-being. 'Tis my duty to ensure ye arrive to Tolton Hall unharmed."

She bowed her head in thanks and moved her gaze to the window. Her attempt to get him talking again had failed. Malcolm was back to treating her formally. It was as if the closer they got to Stonehaven, the tighter his professional hat came on.

Blowing out a breath, she hoped they would arrive at their destination soon. She didn't normally like to mope, but yet, the longer she sat here, in this silent carriage, the more sour her mood got.

When she saw the trees give way to buildings and felt the familiar rumble of cobblestone beneath the carriage wheels, Lizzie breathed a sigh of relief. They had finally arrived in town and would soon be at whatever inn it was that Malcolm deemed appropriate for them to spend the afternoon and night.

As expected, the inn was clean and airy with beautiful decorations. After the accommodations Malcolm had provided previously, she expected naught less. The room she and Mary were assigned was comfortable and spacious. Two beds covered with rose-colored bedding and blue pillows sat on opposite walls. Finally, they each had their own bed. Not that she had minded their shared sleeping arrangements, but it would be nice not to worry about waking Mary if she had another restless night.

Unceremoniously, Lizzie dropped onto one, bouncing on the mattress, her arm covering her eyes.

The bed dipped beside her and Mary patted her leg.

"What bothers ye, Miss? I believe we will arrive home on the morrow. Doesna that make ye happy?"

Lizzie straightened her arms and fisted the duvet. "Nay. I mean, aye, I will be happy to be home. But I dinna look forward to dealing with my parents' wrath. They are going to be most upset with me."

Mary sighed. "Aye, ye will need to put your debating skills to use when that conversation happens," she chided.

Lizzie kenned she was trying to lighten the mood, and she appreciated her maid for doing so. But she still dreaded their arrival.

"I suppose on the bright side, I will be able to prove my innocence to the earl."

"Right. That is a good thing, is it no'?"

She sighed. "'Tis. Do ye think he dislikes me so?"

Mary frowned. "Whye'er do ye ask such a thing?"

"His demeanor today was quite distant. Did ye no' think so? 'Twas much different than previously." She opted not to tell Mary of how attractive she found him when he let down his guard. Or how his deep brogue had her toes curling in her slippers.

"I think he may just have a lot on his mind. Mayhap he is questioning whether or no' ye really are the thief." Mary pulled her to a sitting position. "We both ken ye are no', but he doesna ken aught about ye."

She blew out an exasperated breath and pushed off the bed. She spoke as she looked out the window, taking in the city below. "I was trying to initiate some of that earlier, but he didna bite. I fear he just believes I am a thief and he's ready to be rid of me."

"Ye must stop these negative thoughts, Miss." Mary set about unpacking their bags for the night.

Mary was right, of course. But Lizzie was beginning to think that Malcolm just wanted to get her home and have naught else do with her. Her feelings were all over the place and she didn't quite understand why it bothered her so much. Why she felt she needed his validation, she didn't ken.

For whatever reason, she wanted him to like her. It made no sense.

She watched the passersby with interest and wondered what it would be like to walk down the street on Malcolm's arm. Would they be like the young couple that just entered the bakery across the way, on the hunt for some sweets to share? Or would they be like the family that slowly ambled along, the woman's belly round with child, as a tot walked between them, each of them holding onto one of his tiny hands? She could only imagine the looks they would receive in either scenario. Indeed they would make a dashing pair, she dared to admit.

A plan started to bloom in her mind. She turned with a chuckle and Mary looked at her like she had two heads, her brow raised in question.

Shaking her head, she dismissed the unspoken question with a wave of her hand.

She would get Malcolm to know her. To like her.

Later that night, after Mary had fallen asleep, Lizzie slipped out of bed. Malcolm had reserved the room right next to them, though she wouldna be surprised if he was standing guard outside their door in the hall. Just as he had done in every inn they'd stayed in on this journey.

Pushing her feet into slippers, she pulled on her robe and cinched it at the waist. With one last look over her shoulder to make sure Mary still slept, she opened the door and slipped out into the hall.

As expected, Malcolm was there. He looked positively exhausted with his shoulders slumped as he leaned his back against the door. She couldn't blame him. She could count on her hands the amount of sleep he'd had since they'd left Twynholm.

"Let me guess," Malcolm spoke quietly. "Ye canna sleep and are in search of warm milk?"

Rubbing her hands together, she took a deep breath, trying to tamp down her nerves that had her stomach suddenly in knots.

"I am no'. I was wondering if we might talk?"

His brows furrowed and his mouth turned down into a frown. He straightened as his eyes darted to the door. "Is something wrong?"

Holding her hands out in front of her to calm him down, she shook her head. "Nay, no' at all. All is well. Mary is sleeping like the dead." She laughed and began to pace the floor. "I dinna think traveling sits verra well with her. She finds it tiring."

A smile brightened his face and Malcolm nodded in understanding. "I miss those days." He bent his knee and slung his arm over the top.

"I do feel awfully bad that I am the cause of your lack of sleep."

"Och, Lass. Ye arena. Dinna fash about that. Now, what would ye like to talk about?"

She glanced up and down the hall. The hour was late and she didn't want to wake anyone trying to rest in their rooms.

"May we speak in private? I wouldna want to wake and anger any other patrons here."

He narrowed his eyes, suddenly looking unsure. "What are ye proposing, miss?" He pushed off the floor and stood tall.

She had to crane her neck to look into his eyes. His mention of the word proposing had her stomach doing a flip for no reason at all.

"Mayhap we can speak in your room?"

Leaning his head back against the door, he closed his eyes. He looked pained.

"I dinna believe that is a good idea."

"Well, we canna stand out here and have a conversation, surely."

The thought of someone hearing their exchange was mortifying. Just because there was no one in the hall with them didn't mean that no one was listening. The walls weren't so thick to block all conversation.

"And we most definitely should no' be in my room. By ourselves. With ye unchaperoned."

She put her hands on her hips and huffed out an exasperated breath. "What do ye think is going to happen? Ye are an honorable man. I trust ye. Do ye no' trust yourself?"

"Miss," he warned. "I've no concern with myself. I think I've proven that in our journey up to this point. Havena I?"

He had a point. Even with his bouts of gruffness, he'd been naught but gentlemanlike in his actions toward her.

Two doors down, a man with groggy eyes stuck his balding head out into the hallway. "I dinna care who dishonors who. Go have your conversation somewhere other than the damn hall." He snapped before disappearing inside and shutting the door quietly behind him.

"Shite," Malcolm muttered. "Come on." He grabbed her hand and pulled her into his room.

It looked similar to her room, including the two beds, which at first glance, looked like they were way too small to fit Malcolm's large frame.

He pointed to one of the beds. "Ye sit there. I will stay here." He was clear on the other side of the room, leaning against the wardrobe, ankles crossed. "Now, what did ye want to speak about?"

Her nerves jumped and her heartbeat hastened. She felt the teeniest bit of perspiration break out on her brow. Why was it so hot in here all of a sudden? She smoothed the skirt of her gown with her palms and exhaled slowly.

"I was wondering if I have done something to offend ye?"

He frowned as his eyes clashed with hers. "Why do ye ask such a thing?"

She shrugged. "It seemed like we were enjoying each other's company. Telling each other of our pasts, and then today, ye have been naught but cold."

"Lass, I fear ye forget our places. Just because I'd rather endure the journey with talk instead of suffering it in silence doesna mean that we are friends."

She winced at his words. She couldn't help it. They hurt far more than they should. As if he'd pulled the dagger from his boot and stabbed her in the heart. But he lied. Malcolm Kennedy may be a lot of things that she didn't ken, but she could tell their conversations had been genuine. Why act this way now?

"I dinna believe ye," she said quietly.

"What is there no' to believe? I have given ye no signals of anything but where we stand now."

Forcing herself to her feet, and in a sudden burst of bravado, she closed the distance between them. Stopping mere inches from him. At this closeness, she needed to crane her neck to look into his eyes. Eyes which were focused on something on the wall behind her, stubbornly refusing to meet her gaze.

"Lass," he warned.

With even more bravado, she reached out and placed a hand on his chest.

He hissed and grasped her hand in his, pulling it off of him, but he didn't let go.

"Ye havena any idea what ye are playing with," he warned again, his blue eyes dark.

Straightening her shoulders, she jutted her chin out defiantly. "Why dinna ye show me then?" she asked, her voice sounding odd to her own ears. Embarrassed at her forwardness, she blushed as heat pooled at her center.

Letting go of her hand, he stepped away and instantly she felt the coolness of his absence. She spun and addressed him. "Ye are a verra confusing man, Malcolm Kennedy."

He raised his brow in question but remained silent, his back stiff and straight.

"Ye treat me with kindness, then coldness, then kindness again. Ye park yourself outside my door to keep me safe, but yet want naught to do with me."

"What kind of man would your father think of me if I let any harm come to ye whilst ye were in my care?"

"Bollocks," she cursed.

Malcolm's eyes rounded in surprise as his mouth turned up in a smirk.

Closing the distance between them again, but this time she kept her hands on her hips. "I think ye are being deceitful when it comes to your feelings." There, she said it. Even though he didn't think she noticed, she did. She saw the way he stole glances at her when he thought she wasn't looking or paying attention. She'd seen them all.

His eyes flared and his hand snaked to the back of her neck, pulling her flush to his chest.

A yelp escaped her lips, but she made no move to back away.

"Ye are insufferable, Lizzie Barclay."

And then he dropped his head and his mouth captured hers. The kiss was fierce, not soft. It held all this passion that he could no longer contain and poured it all into this kiss.

And she loved every moment of it. She kenned she shouldn't. It was wrong in so many ways, but God above, she wanted the kiss.

She wrapped her arms around his neck and opened her mouth to his and when his tongue entered her mouth, a thrill shot through her spine. She'd never felt anything like it, and she sighed into his mouth.

He dropped his arms to her waist and his hands cupped her buttocks, pulling her even closer. She gasped as she felt his erection against her stomach.

He broke the kiss, pulling his mouth away from hers, but he kept her pressed against him. His gaze smashed into hers and she noted the blue of his eyes had darkened even deeper than before to the color of the sea on a stormy night.

"Ye are entering dangerous territory, Lass."

CHAPTER THIRTEEN

M ALCOLM STOOD THERE, his cock pressed into Lizzie's stomach and he wanted so much more. Being close to her wasn't enough. He wanted to be buried bollocks deep inside of her sweetness.

And it was wrong.

So wrong.

Every fiber of his being told him to push her away. To leave the room. But he couldn't get himself to do it. It was as if his feet were planted into the floor.

She felt so good molded against him. As if she were made to fit him and only him.

Her erratic breathing matched his own.

"Kiss me again," she whispered, her voice husky, edged with need.

Fuck. As much as he kenned he should be a gentleman and send her on her way. That what they were about to do, because there was no denying what was going to happen, shouldn't happen. They both kenned it would.

But he was the man. He should stop. But he couldn't.

"Malcolm," she called, forcing him to look at her with a soft hand placed against his cheek. As her fingers stroked his skin and then pushed through his hair, she brought his mouth down to hers. Her mouth was open, waiting for him.

And he was lost. Like a man starving, he devoured her mouth as his hands roamed over her body. He found the bow at her waist and pulled at the tie, feeling her robe open.

He paused, because as much as he wanted this, she only had to say nay and he would stop that very second. No question. He would not push her into something she did not want.

"Lizzie?"

"Hmmm," she moaned, her lips red and swollen from their kisses.

"We need to stop."

"I dinna want to." She tried to pull him down to her again, but by something that could only be a miracle, he held back.

"There is nay going back if we continue."

"I understand." The look through her lashes she gave him had his cock weeping.

"Ye will be ruined."

"I dinna care."

He sighed. "I do. Your future husband will verra much care." And that was the thought that did it. As much as he wanted to lose himself in her soft curves, he would not be the cause of her fall from society.

Thief or not, he had more honor than that.

He stepped back, and the look of hurt in her eyes hit him like a punch in the gut.

She reached for him, but he shook his head. "Nay, Lass. We canna. Ye deserve more."

"Let me decide what 'tis I deserve." He saw the tear drop from in the corner of her eye and he had to fight the urge to kiss it away. Guilt consumed him about how selfish he had acted.

He approached her and her eyes brightened. Only to dim once again when he reached forward and cinched her robe closed and tied it off.

"Malcolm," she choked.

"Lass," he moved to the bed and sat down, "come sit, let us talk."

She sat beside him, their arms brushing, and he thought that this wasn't the best idea he'd ever had. He only had to kiss her and lean her back onto the mattress, lift the skirts of her nightdress, drag his hand lazily up her…

"Shite," he snapped and he jumped from the bed as if he'd been burned by the fires of hell itself.

Her pretty mouth formed into an O as she watched him.

"What did I do?"

Pushing his hands through his hair, he paced the floor, moving from one side of the room to the other as she tracked his every step. The room felt too small. He needed more space.

"I fear I am e'en more confused than I was earlier. Do ye havena interest in me?"

He barked out a laugh, the sound filling the room, and he wouldn't be surprised if everyone else staying at the inn had heard it.

"Och, Lass, havena ye seen the effect ye have on me? Didna ye feel it when ye were pressed against me?"

She nodded, wringing her hands in her lap. "Then what is the issue?"

"Ye are an innocent. I willna take that from ye."

She worried her lip, her slippered foot drawing invisible lines on the carpet. "But what if I want to give it to ye. Ye dinna have to take it. I offer it freely."

Her words were soft. Innocent. He groaned. Lizzie was going to be the death of him. War wasn't as dangerous as this lass in his room was. "Ye dinna understand what ye speak of. The consequences it will have on your life. On your future. Your chances to secure a husband."

"What if I dinna want a husband? Or what if I do and I ken who 'tis?"

"Christ. Ye are already promised to someone?" Jesus, it was a good thing he'd gotten his wits about him when he did. Otherwise, he'd be dueling at dawn against someone he'd never met. She was full of surprises.

"Nay!" She hopped up from the bed and sidled toward him, her hips swaying back and forth in the most seductive way.

Damn, she was good. For a woman with no experience, she could give some of the more experienced women he'd lost himself in before a run for their money. Whether it was her innocence that propelled her forward or instinct, he didn't know. But it was breaking him. The walls he'd constructed were starting to crumble. His defenses were being battered and he feared defeat was in his future.

For the first time in his life.

"Mayhap ye could be my husband," she said innocently, her cheeks a beautiful pink.

"I canna."

"Why no'?" She stopped in front of him, looking up through her long, dark lashes. Her chocolate brown eyes shining in the candlelight.

"Because I belong to no one. I'm nobody's man. Or husband."

She tilted her head, her tongue darting out and wetting her lips and his cock about punched through his pants. He groaned, unable to contain himself.

"But ye could be," she said quietly. "Who's stopping ye?"

He had to stop and think about that for a long moment. Who was stopping him? Other than himself. He'd always told himself he would be alone. It was easier belonging to nobody than tangling himself in a relationship.

But the halls of Culzean were awfully quiet. Certainly, he hadn't met anyone in Edinburgh that he found interesting enough to want to spend more than a night with.

But Lizzie? He could picture her curled up on the chaise lounge in front of the fireplace in his library, reading a book, while he sat in his chair, smoking a pipe whilst he read the paper.

The image was clear as day in his mind, and it caused him to suck in his breath sharply.

"What is it?" Lizzie asked, concern creasing her forehead. "I didna mean to upset ye. I apologize." She threw her arms up in the air. "I have no idea what I am doing obviously. I guess I thought I had seen something that wasna there."

Throwing his head back, he bit back a groan. What she thought was true. He just wasn't ready to admit it to himself.

He was being a cad. And he kenned it.

She moved to the door, and he hurried over to it, blocking her exit.

"Lass," he whispered, his voice low.

"Aye?" She said, her arms crossed in front of her breasts. Breasts that he wanted to see so badly. Breasts that he yearned to cup in his hands, kenning they would be the perfect fit for his palms.

"I dinna want ye to go," he confessed. His mind screamed at him that he was wrong, but his heart. His body. They both cheered in triumph as she sank into his arms and he scooped her up as if his very life depended on it.

His mouth found hers once again and he savored the taste of her. She tasted of the ripest, sweetest berry, and he was a starving man.

The way she clung to him had him feeling like he never wanted her to let go.

He broke the kiss and pushed off the door, carrying Lizzie to the bed where he gently laid her down.

She looked up at him, her big brown eyes hooded.

Steps sounded outside the door and the intrusion shook him out of whatever hold the lass had on him. It was as if she were a witch, casting a spell upon him. He sat up and rested his head in his hands.

"I canna do it, Lass."

A small hand clutched his shoulder, and she pulled herself up. Lizzie settled in beside him, her body warm against his.

"I want ye, too," she said quietly.

He shook his head. "I canna. I will no' ruin ye to satisfy my wants. Or your wants. Ye deserve better."

The words killed him as they left his mouth. Never had he put so much effort into not bedding a lass. It was taking all of his willpower and the longer she looked at him with hunger in her eyes, the more he wanted to push her onto the bed and tup her right there.

He stood and offered her his hand. When she clasped it, her fingers curling around his, he pulled her up. "Come on, Lass. Let's get ye back to your own room."

Without a word, she nodded and let him lead her out into the hall.

At her door, he paused.

"Lass, if our situation were different, 'twould be nay hesitation on my part. Ye are a beautiful woman that deserves the world." He tucked a wayward curl behind her ear, letting his fingers trail slowly down her cheek.

And then, not trusting himself to keep his word, he quickly spun on his heel, disappearing into his own room, and locking the door, trying not to pay attention to Lizzie standing there looking dejected.

PUSHING OPEN THE door to her room, Lizzie entered and closed it behind her. Mary still slept. Lizzie was amazed she didn't hear any of the actions outside their room. To her ears it seemed like they were making enough noise to raise the dead.

Her skin still tingled from all of Malcolm's touches. She didn't want him to stop, and she'd be lying if his words didn't hurt.

They did.

She slipped into bed and buried her head in the pillow. Wishing for sleep to overtake her so she could escape all the emotions running wild through her body.

After tossing and turning for the next hour, sleep, finally overtook her.

"Miss." Lizzie woke to the sound of Mary's voice and a gentle shaking. "'Tis time to wake. We must make haste. 'Tis late."

Lizzie groaned and rubbed the sleep out of her eyes. She was exhausted. "What time is it?"

"The earl is waiting for us in the hall."

Really? Had she really slept so late?

"I thought something was amiss with ye. I tried waking ye earlier and there was no rousing ye."

She wasn't ready to face Malcolm. Her limbs felt heavy and she wanted naught more than to curl up and burrow herself under the covers.

His rejection was embarrassing.

"Come on, Miss."

Mary unceremoniously yanked the duvet down and Lizzie groaned.

"Fine!" she blurted. "Since ye willna cease."

Her maid giggled. "We've no time. Ye dinna want to keep the earl waiting any longer, do ye?"

Actually, she did, but she couldn't tell Mary that. If her maid learned how close she had come to giving herself to the earl last night, she would have her head.

Then she would tell her parents what she'd done, and they would insist that the earl make things right and take responsibility for his actions.

Yet, she felt she was the one pushing more. Aye, he felt the same as her, but he had much more self-control.

Much more.

And in the light of a new day, she realized he was right in sending her back to her room. Not that she would have regretted it. She wouldn't have. But she understood the repercussions of what almost happened.

As much as she didn't want to admit it, Malcolm was right. When she saw him later, she would thank him. It was stupid. He'd probably think she was daft but, truly, she was grateful that he was able to keep his wits about him.

One of them had to.

Because she definitely had not.

After freshening up and dressing in a light-yellow day dress with a green sash tied at her waist, Lizzie opened the door to a waiting Malcolm. His eyes flared at the sight of her. Proof that his feelings were there. The butterflies in her stomach fluttered to life and her pulse quickened.

Not trusting her voice, she nodded her greeting, and they made their way downstairs and out to the carriage.

Today they would finally arrive at Tolton Hall. She was both excited and weary about seeing her parents again. Certainly, this would be the last time they ever let her travel alone again. For that she was sure.

She'd broken their trust. They wouldn't take kindly to that. She'd probably be locked in her room until they felt she'd learned her lesson. But on the bright side, today was also the day she would prove to Malcolm that she wasn't a thief.

And she would get her grandmother's jewelry back. Where it rightfully belonged.

Malcolm cleared his throat behind her. "Lass, may I have a word?"

She turned to look at him, and in his eyes was that same longing from the night before. One that matched her own.

"Of course." She stepped back from the carriage and Mary went to follow, but she waved her away. "We willna be far, Mary. Dinna fash. We will stay within eyesight."

"Aye, Miss." Mary curtsied and hung back as Malcolm guided Lizzie by the elbow and they walked away out of earshot.

He blew out an exasperated breath before speaking. He looked like he was searching for the right words to say. He also looked like he hadn't slept a wink last night. His blond hair wasn't brushed as neatly as it usually was. And dark circles formed under his eyes.

She stayed silent, her hands clasped in front of her as she watched a flood of emotions cross his handsome face.

"About last night..."

"Och." She clucked her tongue and waved his words away. "Please, my lord. We needn't discuss what transpired. Or did no' transpire," she added, a bit playfully to the lighten the mood which had grown heavy when they left Mary.

He chuckled, running a hand through his thick hair, causing it to stand on end. "I appreciate ye saying such words. I would like ye to ken that if circumstances were different, I would court ye in a heartbeat. Which, if ye kenned my past, ye would understand how much that means."

She licked her lips and caught the way his eyes tracked to her mouth, his pupils flaring. Tilting her head to the side, she put her hands on her hips. "Ye are welcome to tell me about how great a feat that is. Because right now, I am sorry to say that I dinna understand." She took in a deep breath before continuing. "But one thing I can tell ye, because I can understand it, is that last night there were plenty of sparks shared betwixt us. And while I may no' be experienced in such things, I dinna consider myself a dolt."

His eyes rounded. "I would ne'er say such a thing." For a moment it looked like he was going to reach for her hand, but his gaze shot back to where Mary was standing, watching their every move and he dropped his hand to his side.

"Ye are a verra lovely lass. Whoe'er ye marry will be verra lucky to have ye."

"Whilst I appreciate your niceties, my lord, your words leave me just as confused as last night." Lizzie had never thought of herself as being particularly forward with men, or anyone really, but she found when it came to Malcolm, she couldn't hold back. "'Twould be nice if ye would give me the benefit of an explanation of what ye meant earlier. Ye are correct I ken naught of your past. But I would like to. If ye would only open up to me. But instead ye hold back. Ye dangle a wee glimpse of what things could be like in front of me, and when I make the jump to accept, ye pull it away. Why?"

CHAPTER FOURTEEN

W HY, INDEED? MALCOLM couldn't explain his actions to himself, how was he supposed to explain them to Lizzie as she looked up at him with her big brown eyes and naught but expectation shining bright within their depths.

Och, how his best friends would laugh at him now and the predicament he found himself in.

He feared that after they got to Tolton Hall this evening and he uncovered the truth, finally, that he would have to give up his investigative work forever. For most certainly he had failed on this mission. He'd kenned it before they even left Twynholm, he just didn't want to admit it to himself.

Lizzie had caught his attention from the first moment their eyes had met from across the hall, and he had been unable to shake the grip she had on him since.

Hell, he'd get down on his damned knee right now and propose to the lass if he could.

But he couldn't. Right now she was infatuated with him. But she didn't ken him. Didn't ken his past. What he'd done. The life he lived before. The number of lasses he'd bedded and then left in the morning so as not to give them any inclination that he had any interest that went further than the hours they'd shared the night before. He'd ruined so many lasses and it never bothered him.

Until Lizzie. The mere thought of taking her innocence for a night of heaven and then walking away, seemed like the worst thing he could do. The thought actually made him sick. And that was why he was wondering what the hell was the matter with him.

"My lord?" Lizzie placed a small hand on his arm, bringing him back to the present, and without thinking, he placed his hand on hers, his thumb rubbing over her knuckles in a gentle caress.

He kenned Mary was watching them. That she could see what they were doing, and he cared naught.

And that was why, right there, in the middle of the street, for anyone to see, he tugged on Lizzie's hand, pulling her close, and captured her mouth to his.

For the briefest of moments, she stiffened in surprise, but then melted into his arms.

The kiss was deep. Passionate. And if they weren't in the middle of the street, he would find himself in much the same predicament that he had last night. Thankfully, the bustle of the streets around them kept his actions in check from going any further. But he also kenned, just kissing her in such a public place was putting her reputation at risk.

He broke the kiss, and Lizzie sighed as she looked at him with hooded eyes and flushed cheeks.

"I have been wanting to do that since ye opened your door, Lass."

She bit her bottom lip and then burst out in laughter. It was contagious, and he soon followed suit. Soon, they were both laughing maniacally in the street and people passing by were giving them odd looks and a wide clearance.

Mary rushed forth. "Sir!" She called. "Miss!" She had her skirts in her fists as she ran towards them. "What are ye doing?" She questioned when she stopped in front of them, her chest heaving. "My lord, pardon me for saying, but that was most improper. And in front of e'eryone no less. Are ye trying to ruin her reputation?"

Beside him, Lizzie giggled. "Mary, cease. We are fine."

"Ye arena. No' at all. Your parents—"

"Willna ken," Lizzie interjected, her voice authoritative. "Unless I want them to, and at this time I am uncertain of that. 'Twas just a kiss. Is that no' right, my lord?" she asked, looking at him innocently, batting her long lashes.

He cleared his throat and straightened. "No disrespect was meant, Mary. I assure ye."

Did the lass really mean it was just a kiss? Or was she saying that for Mary's sake? Once again, he questioned his sleuthing skills, because he couldn't deduce whether Lizzie was being genuine or not. Lord help him.

"The hour grows late. Let us continue our journey and we'll make it to Tolton Hall by late afternoon."

Lizzie's demeanor changed at the mention of her home. "Are ye no' excited to go home, Lass?" He bent and whispered close to her ear, the temptation to dare nip her lobe with his teeth strong.

She shrugged her shoulders as they walked toward the carriage. "I am. I do miss my parents, but no' the wrath I will face once they find out what I have done. Also, I'll be happy to prove to ye that those jewels ye are keeping from me are mine once and for all."

He nodded and helped her into the carriage. Then Mary, and he followed behind, settling into the bench across from them.

Lizzie stuck out a foot and nudged his boot discreetly.

He raised a brow in question, and she just laughed as the carriage lurched forward and they were on their way.

IT WAS ALMOST suppertime when the carriage rocked to a halt in front of the steps of Tolton Hall. It was a beautiful building that looked out to the North Sea. He imagined if they went out the back door of the estate, their feet would meet pebbly sand and hear the rush of the waves as they crashed to shore.

A woman rushed out the front door, and from the resemblance to Lizzie, Malcolm expected the woman was her mama.

"You're back," she exclaimed happily when Lizzie exited the carriage, pulling her into a warm embrace. "Did ye have a nice visit?"

"Mama, please," Lizzie begged, embarrassment tinging her cheeks bright pink.

The woman gave a kind smile to Mary as she stepped from the carriage, and then her eyes widened when Malcolm exited.

"Och, who do we have here?" Her hand fluttered to the pendant she wore and she started fidgeting with the gem, her eyes darting to Lizzie.

"Mama, this is Lord Kennedy, Earl of Cassilis. Sir, this is my mama, Lydia, Baroness Barclay."

Malcolm stepped forward and bowed. "'Tis verra nice to make your acquaintance. I have heard much about ye."

Lydia's brows drew together as she gave her daughter a questioning look. But Lizzie just ignored her.

"Well, I am sure ye have had a long journey. Please, come inside." She snaked her hand into the crook of Lizzie's elbow. "I am curious to ken what is happening."

Inside, Malcolm was ushered to the salon and offered refreshments. He took a seat and waited for the inevitable arrival of Mr. Barclay. Any man worth his salt would want to assess the man that had shown up with his unmarried daughter, with her maid as her only chaperone.

He wasn't sure what he would tell them yet. He thought it was only proper that Lizzie explained exactly what happened first. He wouldn't implicate her in any way.

The last thing he wanted to do was put her in a bad light with her parents.

While he waited, he got up and paced around the room, studying the many portraits hanging on the walls.

And that was when he saw it.

The portrait of what could only be Lizzie's grandmama. The resemblance was unmistakable. They had the same coloring, along with the same eyes.

And smile.

They both had beautiful smiles. But that wasn't what caught his attention. Nay, what his eyes focused on was the necklace she wore.

He reached into his pocket and pulled out the pouch he'd stored the necklace in when he'd requested it back from Lizzie, and held it up, studying it against the portrait.

Well, shite.

Lizzie *had* been telling him the truth this whole time. It also proved that it wasn't Lizzie that robbed the estate on the first night they'd stopped. That truly had been the Phantom Prowler... most likely the viscountess as Lizzie had suspected. Which he had kenned all along. The more time he'd spent with her, the more he realized she couldn't be the prowler.

He didn't think the lass had a deceptive bone in her body. Well, except for her wee deception of her parents, that is.

And she'd be dealing with whatever punishment they deemed fit soon enough. He hoped they wouldn't be too hard on the lass. Her motive was genuine, and she only had her family's best interest at heart.

"Lord Malcolm, welcome to Tolton Hall." Richard Barclay entered the room and held out his hand for a shake.

He dropped the necklace into his pocket.

"Sir Barclay. I thank ye for the welcome."

"I think 'tis I that should be thanking ye."

Malcolm raised his brow in question.

"For getting my daughter home safely to us. Though, I would like to learn the details of how that came to be."

It was a question disguised as a statement, but Malcolm didn't take the bait. He wouldn't give Lizzie up. She had made the decisions she had, and it was up to her to explain them to her parents, not him.

"DID YE SEE the portrait?" Lizzie asked Malcolm as she burst into the room.

He and her papa were talking in hushed tones, and they turned to look at her. Papa looked confused, but Malcolm kenned exactly what she was asking.

"What portrait?" her mama asked, following her in.

Lizzie pointed to the wall where her grandmama's portrait hung high in the center. The jewelry she'd recovered from the viscountess, hanging around her grandmama's neck and dangling from her lobes.

Mama's eyes tracked to the portrait, and she frowned.

"Why would Lord Malcolm have any interest in our family portraits?"

"No' our family portraits, Mama. Just Grandmama's portrait."

Her mama held her hands up. "I believe I am missing something." She looked at Papa. "Do ye ken what our daughter is talking about?"

Papa shook his head. "I havena any clue. Lizzie, dear, what is this all about?"

Lizzie sighed as she bit her bottom lip. Now was the time that she needed to tell her parents what she'd done. Three sets of eyes focused on her and the room felt suddenly hot and small. As if the walls were closing in on her.

"Lizzie," her papa drawled, "I ken ye too well. Ye are hiding something. Let's all have a seat and ye can tell us all about it."

She scrunched her face. She wasn't so sure she really wanted to do that. But as her parents looked at her expectantly, she sighed and dropped into a chair, fidgeting with the satin sash of her gown.

Her eyes clashed with Malcolm's and he gave the slightest nod of his head, urging her to tell her parents what she'd done.

Taking a deep breath, she started. "First, I would like to say that I understand that ye will be upset with me, however, I also would like ye to ken that I only did it to retrieve what had been stolen from us."

Both her mama and papa's brows drew down in confusion. "I havena the slightest idea of what ye speak of, Lizzie, but ye have us intrigued. Lord Kennedy, I assume ye are aware?"

Malcolm nodded. "I've an inkling."

Her papa focused on her once again. "Well, we are waiting." He crossed his legs and leaned back in his chair.

"Also, please dinna be angry with Mary. She was only doing what I asked of her. She is verra loyal and deserves to be rewarded, no' disciplined."

Her father crossed his arms, his mouth dipped down in a frown as he regarded her. He didn't look happy.

She swallowed the lump in her throat and confessed to all she had done.

How she lied about visiting a friend.

How she took the Wilson's invitation and went to the party.

And how she recovered her grandmama's jewelry.

"Lizzie," her mother said, her voice dripping with disappointment. "What have ye done?"

"I took what rightly belonged to me. To us. It canna be stealing if they were ours to begin with."

"And ye caught her in the act?" Papa asked Malcolm, his voice serious.

"Aye. Though I must admit, I didna take the lass for a thief. Especially the Phantom Prowler. She was much too loud and careless for that," he said with a small smile.

Papa chuckled, but Mama's mouth stayed in a thin line. "Ye are truly daft, Lizzie. How could ye take such risks for, for that?"

"Why wouldna I? 'Tis Grandmama's jewelry. It belongs to me. She gifted it to me," she said stubbornly. Why couldn't they see what was happening? Her intentions were true.

Mama pinched the bridge of her nose between her thumb and index finger. "Aside from the fact of how ye thought ye would find them at the Wilsons' home, which is an issue we will deal with later, ye risked e'erything for colored glass."

Now it was Lizzie's turn to be confused. "What are ye speaking of?"

"The gems, Lizzie. They are fake," her mother explained in exasperation.

"But those pieces were Grandmama's favorites. She wore them all the time."

"Aye, she did. Because she thought the designer had done such fine work on them. They fooled e'eryone. Including ye, apparently. But they're worth naught."

Well, color her a fool. She felt her face flame in embarrassment. Her grandmama's jewels were fake. She shook her head in disbelief. It didn't matter in the end. She wasn't after the jewels because they were worth a lot of coin. She was after them because they belonged to her grandmama. And then someone came into their house and stole them.

Stole what was rightfully hers.

She was only righting the wrong that had been done against them.

Her gaze clashed with Malcolm's. He was watching her closely as he slipped a hand into his jacket pocket. When he withdrew it, her grandmama's jewels were in his palm, which he held out for her to take.

Tentatively, she took a step forward. When her parents didn't move to stop her, she closed the distance and scooped the jewels from Malcolm's palm, cradling them to her chest. It was like hugging an old friend.

It didn't matter that the gems weren't real. What mattered were the memories the jewelry represented. Memories of Lizzie watching

Grandmama ready herself for a party or a ball. Of her grandmama's nimble fingers clasping the necklace around her slender neck and latching the earrings into each lobe. Grandmama would regale Lizzie with stories from her past. She reveled in those memories.

And the jewelry played a large part in each one.

Even now, with them cupped in her palms, she felt her grandmama's presence. That was all she cared about.

"Lizzie," Papa called, drawing her attention back to the present. "We have much to discuss with Lord Kennedy. We will decide upon proper punishment later. Until then, go to your room." Her father turned his back to her, effectively dismissing her as if she were a petulant child.

Malcolm frowned but said naught.

Embarrassed that she was being treated like a child, especially in front of Malcolm, she refused to meet his eyes. Instead, she dropped her head and left the room.

Fighting back tears, she made her way upstairs as the doors to the salon clicked shut.

CHAPTER FIFTEEN

MALCOLM WATCHED LIZZIE hurry out the door, and it took all of his strength not to chase after her and crush her in his arms. He wanted to whisper in her ear that everything would be all right.

She looked crushed when her father told her to leave the room, and it hit Malcolm like a punch in the gut.

He noticed Mrs. Barclay assessing his gaze as he tracked Lizzie. Her brows lifted in curiosity when their eyes met, but he said naught.

"So, Lord Kennedy," Sir Barclay stated, oblivious to what his wife had just observed. "I would like to ken how ye came to be acquainted with our daughter?"

His voice was stern, and Malcolm couldn't blame him for his countenance. If an unknown man arrived on his doorstep escorting his unmarried daughter, he would also be upset.

Malcolm cleared his throat. His nerves did a wee jump. He almost laughed. Of all the situations he had found himself in previously, this was by far the least dangerous, and the most innocent, but yet he found himself more nervous than ever.

A niggling thought entered his mind.

Ye ken what this means. Ye like the lass.

If he didn't have Lizzie's parents looking at him and waiting for him to answer the question, he might have laughed at the absurdity.

She was just a job.

And he was just a fool if he actually believed that.

"My lord?" Sir Barclay pushed.

"Ah, yes. Apologies."

Mrs. Barclay gave him a small smile but remained silent.

"We, Miss Lizzie and I, met at the Wilsons' party at which we were both in attendance."

"Do ye ken the viscount well?"

Malcolm shrugged. "We have kenned each other for quite some time. He hired my services to ensure the safety of their jewels from the Phantom Prowler—if he happened to show up."

"Did he?" Sir Barclay asked.

Malcolm chuckled. "No' in the verra least. As a matter of fact, I was making one last round of the Wilson estate afore taking my leave for the night. I happened to hear noise coming from the viscountess's bedchamber and, kenning she was downstairs, there should have been no-one in the room." He paused before continuing on. "When I investigated—"

"Investigated? Are ye a detective, Lord Kennedy?" Mrs. Barclay asked.

"Nay." He shook his head. "I've just done this line of work for quite some time, so Wilson called me in. As I was saying, whilst investigating the source of the noise, I came upon Miss Lizzie. In the viscountess's chamber, her hands deep in the lady's jewel chest."

Mrs. Barclay gasped, her hand moving to fidget once again with the pendant hanging at her neck. "Ye think our Lizzie is the Phantom Prowler? She has ne'er done aught as this. She is a good girl."

"Och, I have nay doubt—"

Mrs. Barclay sucked in a breath.

"—that Miss Lizzie is no' the Phantom Prowler."

The baroness let out a long breath of relief, but then turned serious. "But ye caught her stealing?"

Malcolm smiled sheepishly. "Aye, I did. And straightaway, Miss Lizzie tried to explain away her actions. She mentioned her grandma-ma, and how the jewelry belonged to her and she was only reclaiming it."

"Oh, well, that's a relief."

"Ye didna turn her into the viscount?" Sir Barclay asked.

"I could do nay such thing. Your daughter was verra vehement in insisting that she was no' the prowler, and that she could prove it." He pointed to the picture that Lizzie told him would prove her innocence.

"She stated that I only needed to set eyes upon this portrait and that she would be proven innocent. She made a verra believable plea. And, dare I say, that the amount of noise she was making trying to find her grandmama's jewels would most definitely rule her out of being the prowler. The prowler was aptly named Phantom as no one kenned he was there. I couldna say that about Miss Lizzie. Which is a good thing," he added.

"Howe'er, I did need her to prove her case. At one point in our travels, a nearby estate was robbed. I would be remiss if I didna confess that there was a moment, I thought Lizzie was playing me for a fool. 'Tis why I am here."

"Well," Mrs. Barclay said. "Now that that has been cleared up, we can move on."

"No' quite so fast," Sir Barclay chimed in. "I am glad ye have concluded our Lizzie is no' the Phantom Prowler and that her intentions were pure. What is no' clear, is why did Lizzie believe she would find the jewels at the viscount's estate? Why were they at the estate in the viscountess's jewelry chest?"

"Ye may be best to ask this question of Miss Lizzie. I asked her the same."

Sir Barclay assessed Malcolm as if to verify he was telling the truth. Malcolm kept a straight face, his mouth set in a firm line that offered no argument. He'd been scrutinized by far more threatening men in his lifetime. Though admittedly, not by any of whom when he found their daughter incredibly enticing.

Sir Barclay sighed. "I suppose we shall ask her." He called for Mary and they waited in silence for the maid to arrive. When she did, he ordered her to collect Lizzie and have her rejoin them in the salon.

"Whilst we wait, may I offer ye tea, my lord?"

"I am fine, thank ye." He thrummed his fingers along the wooden arm of the chair he sat in as he waited for Lizzie to reappear.

When she entered the room, Malcolm's heart tugged. She looked defeated. Gone was the sassy, chipper lass that he'd gotten to ken over their journey to Tolton Hall. Guilt assuaged him. He couldn't help feeling that he was to blame.

"Ah, Lizzie. Please have a seat," her father ordered.

She hurried to an empty chair and gracefully folded into it.

"It has been confirmed that ye couldna possibly be the Phantom Prowler."

Lizzie rolled her eyes as if that were obvious.

"Howe'er, how did ye ken ye would find your grandmama's jewelry at the Wilson's?"

Malcolm sat quietly as he listened to Lizzie explain how she figured out Viscountess Wilson was the Phantom Prowler. Her explanation now was the same as it was, when he'd asked her the same question.

"But I dinna want to get the viscountess in trouble. No' at all. I did what I set out to do."

Finally, not able to remain silent any longer, Malcolm spoke up. "Ye realize what ye have done?" he asked Lizzie.

Her gaze flew to his, worry darkening the irises. "I-I dinna ken," she said quietly.

Smiling, he pushed off the chair and walked to the far side of the room, then turned to face the Barclays. "All of Scotland is on the Phantom Prowler case, who, by the way, is widely believed to be male. Ye have succeeded in what they have failed. Ye identified the prowler."

Lizzie shook her head. "That is no' what I was trying to do. I only wanted—"

Malcolm held up his hand. "I ken, ye only wanted to retrieve what was rightfully yours. Which ye did, but also, in the process, ye uncovered the thief. Something some of the most qualified investigators have been unable to do."

"I willna say a word or turn her into the authorities. The viscountess is a family friend. Has been for as long as I can remember. But I willna ruin her life. E'en if she stole what was most precious to me."

He admired her determination to keep her family friend safe, even when that friend put her own freedom in jeopardy.

"Was the viscount made aware of Lizzie's actions?"

Malcolm shook his head. "Absolutely no'. I gave no inclination whatsoe'er as to what Miss Lizzie had been up to."

"Well, whilst I am proud of ye for uncovering the thief, I am no' happy with the way ye went about it. Howe'er, I have no intention of bringing any related attention to our family, so I will leave ye do to what ye will with the information regarding the viscountess, Lord Kennedy." Sir Barclay sat back in his chair and pierced him with a serious look.

"Now, onto the subject of my daughter. Ye have traveled the countryside with her. Alone."

"Papa," Lizzie chimed in. "We werena alone. Mary was with us at all times."

"Aye, so instead of traveling with one young girl alone, he's traveled with two. That is much better."

Malcolm pushed off the wall, the urge to clench his hands into fists strong. His voice low, he addressed Barclay. "Dinna speak aloud what ye are thinking, I warn ye. Ye forget who ye are speaking to. I would ne'er compromise the innocence of a lass. And I'm offended that ye would say such a thing."

Sir Barclay clenched his jaw as he held Malcolm's gaze. It felt like he was trying to read his very soul. And if he could, he would see that Malcolm had not harmed the lass.

Had he crossed a line? Aye. By kissing her, he most definitely had. But he would not admit to doing so and put Lizzie in a compromising position.

Apparently, believing what he saw, Barclay looked away with a nod.

"The hour grows late, my lord. I insist that ye stay the night. 'Tis no' safe to travel the roads at night," Mrs. Barclay declared. Her eyes darted to Lizzie and then back to him. "Besides, 'tis been a long day cooped up in the carriage and then in the house, I think a stroll around the estate would do ye and Lizzie some good," she prompted.

"Dearest?" Sir Barclay questioned.

She dismissed his question with a wave of her hand. "They can take Mary as chaperone if 'twill make ye feel better. I doubt the earl would try to defile our daughter on a walk of our grounds."

Lizzie gasped from her chair. "Mama!"

"Och, please. Go," Mrs. Barclay ordered, shooing her hands in front of her. "Outside with ye both." She nodded her head in Malcolm's direction, then dropped into a curtsy. "My lord."

LIZZIE HAD NO idea what had overcome her mama. It was so very far out of character for her mama to sweep them out the door for a walk.

Yet, here she found herself, outside with the earl. Her arm linked into his as they walked the path outside the estate that would bring them close to the sea. As ordered, Mary followed behind them at a safe distance.

"Your mama is a feisty woman," Malcolm commented, breaking the silence.

"Aye. I dinna ken what came over her."

"Indeed, but I shan't complain."

She looked up to see him smiling down at her. "Careful, Papa is already suspicious of ye and your actions."

Malcolm barked out a laugh. "My actions? Whate'er do ye speak of?"

She bumped her shoulder into his side. "Thank ye for no' mentioning the kiss. Or kisses. Papa would be most upset with that information."

"I would ne'er do or say anything to put ye in an ill light. I promise ye that."

The rocky pathway gave way to pebbly sand, making Lizzie's steps unsteady. Malcolm's arm tightened, pulling her closer to ensure she didn't fall.

Worrying her lip with her teeth, she thought of how to voice what was running rampant through her mind. He might think her silly. But she wanted him to ken. To understand how she felt.

"I must confess, I verra much liked your kisses." She felt her face flame at her confession. Their eyes met and the heat in his gaze sent shivers up and down her spine. It gave her the confidence to continue. "Ye illicit feelings in me that I've ne'er experienced afore."

"Lass."

The word was almost a moan as it fell from his full lips, drawing her attention to them. Was it wrong that she wanted him to kiss her again? Wrong that she longed for the feel of his touch? She was certain that the feelings were shared between the two of them. His reaction to her was just as strong as she to him.

With a glance over her shoulder to see where Mary was, she pulled Malcolm into an ivy-covered alcove.

"Lass, we canna do this," Malcolm pleaded, as if he was physically in pain.

"Kiss me," she ordered, her voice sounding stronger than she felt. She waited, holding her breath to see what he would do.

His facial expressions went from concern, to surprise, to his eyes flaring with heat.

"Mary will see. And I willna put ye in a position ye later regret."

His ethics were commendable. But she didn't want ethics. Didn't want nice. She wanted Malcolm's lips on hers.

And naught would appease her.

"I promise ye 'tis no' something I will regret." She grasped his lapels and pulled him closer. "Now, afore Mary arrives, kiss me as I asked."

His pupils blew wide at her words.

Mayhap she was being too forward. It was most unladylike, but when it came to Malcolm Kennedy, she could not help herself.

Losing his fight of self-control, Malcolm lowered his head and captured her lips in a searing kiss that had her toes curling in her walking slippers.

She clung to her shoulders for if she didn't, she would surely lose her ability to stand. She savored the feel of him flush against her. Savored the taste of him. She wanted the kiss to last forever.

But much too quickly, Malcolm broke the kiss, straightening to full height, and yanked at his cravat as he cleared his throat.

"Lizzie."

She loved when he called her by her name without the "Miss" in front of it.

"Ye are playing with fire, Lass." He pulled her back onto the walking path just as Mary caught up to them. "The creeping ivy is lovely," he stated, admirably trying to conceal the reason they were in the alcove in the first place.

Mary knotted her brows, but said naught.

They continued on their walk, keeping their voices low so as not to allow Mary to hear their conversation.

"I would verra much like to be greeted that way e'ery time we meet."

He patted the hand she had resting in the crook of his elbow. "As much as I would like to fulfill your request, I dinna believe your father would be quite happy with that." He winked at her and her knees nearly buckled.

"But, would ye like it?" she asked.

His gaze was serious as he looked at her. "I would, Lass. Verra much so."

It was as if the good lord above had shined his very light upon her. Inside her chest, her heart swelled.

Gathering her courage once again, she pushed forward. "Ye could speak to Papa," she suggested hopefully.

They came upon a bench set against a trellis wall of more creeping ivy and Malcolm pulled her over to sit upon it.

Mary stopped walking and held her distance, but still kept an eye on them. Lizzie was still amazed she hadn't rushed forward when they'd disappeared into the alcove.

Malcolm's brows furrowed, his lips pressed together as he appeared to mull over what he wanted to say.

She folded her hands on her lap and waited patiently. Is this when he called her a young lass with a head full of childhood dreams? Even though he said he wanted to kiss her every day didn't mean that he would be willing to accept the commitment such a task would require. They hadn't spoke of a courtship previously. Would they now?

"Tell me what your future looks like."

The question was most unexpected. It was her turn to grow serious. Truth be told, she saw him in her future. Them building a home together. Raising a family together. Did she dare say as much? Her stomach clenched in a knot. Telling Malcolm that she wanted to be greeted by his kisses every day was one thing. But actually telling him that she wanted to build a life with him? That could be too much.

And the last thing she wanted to feel was his rejection.

But, she'd confessed so much already. Been so improperly forward already, why should she stop now?

A breeze swirled around them, blowing loose a tendril of hair that she swiped away and tucked behind her ear.

"If I am being honest, I see ye in my future. I think I have pictured it since the moment I first laid eyes upon ye. Afore ye found me in the viscountess's chambers. I'm no' sure if ye remember, but our eyes had met afore then."

He nodded. "Aye, I remember. I remember seeing the most beautiful eyes I'd e'er had the pleasure to lay sight upon."

Again, her stomach flip-flopped. She couldn't stop the huge smile that spread across her face.

"I canna forget that moment."

"Nor can I." He smiled warmly. "With that being said, I believe the only thing that I can do from this point forward is to woo ye by courting ye. If ye'll have me, of course."

CHAPTER SIXTEEN

MALCOLM WAITED ON bated breath like a lad daring his first kiss. What the hell had him so unsure of himself? Surely, this is what his friends felt when they'd come to the realization that they'd met the woman they wanted to spend the rest of their lives with.

And that was exactly what he wanted to do with Lizzie.

He watched the rise and fall of her chest as she absorbed what he'd proposed. Her face breaking into a beautiful smile that the devil himself wouldn't be able to steal away.

She bobbed her head up and down before throwing her arms around his neck. He inhaled the scent of her as he wrapped his arms around her waist.

Mary stepped forward to intervene, but he stopped her with a wave of her hand and then unwound himself from Lizzie's embrace.

"Afore we have any such displays as this, I must speak to your father."

Her lower lip jutted out in a pout, but she nodded her head in agreement.

"Ye've a point. Mayhap we should make our way inside so that ye may have the necessary discussion?"

Thirty minutes later, Sir Barclay ushered Malcolm into his study and pointed to a chair for him to take a seat.

"Whisky?" he asked.

Malcolm nodded. Who was he to turn down a good dram? He'd be daft to do so.

"Thank ye," he said as he took the glass and swirled the amber liquid in the crystal glass he'd been given.

Barclay took a seat behind his desk and leaned back, crossing his legs. "I've been informed that ye have something important to discuss with me." He paused, waiting patiently for Malcolm to speak.

Malcolm cleared his throat and tilted his head from side to side, trying to relieve the tension that had built up in his neck. It was stupid really. Considering he was a grown man. He'd served in the war for Christ's sake.

How did this wisp of a lass bring him to his knees?

Her charm. Her wit. Her beauty. And as much as it was not the proper countenance, her forwardness. He absolutely loved that about her. That she wasn't scared to tell him what she felt. What she wanted. He found it absolutely enticing.

"In the past several days that I have spent with your daughter, I have found myself inexplicably drawn to her. She's smart, and beautiful, with a personality I've no' oft seen."

Barclay raised a brow in question at the last part of his statement.

"That is in nay means an insult, sir. I find it quite," he paused, searching for the correct word, "refreshing. All of this to say that I would like your blessing to court your daughter."

He waited, not realizing he held his breath until Barclay gave him his blessing and his breath rushed out in a huff.

"Of course, she has a dowry, but I suspect that ye are well enough established that 'tis no' of need or plays any part in ye asking for the courtship."

"'Tis true. I am in nay need of any monetary gains from Lizzie. Whate'er coin or land she currently holds as dowry will remain hers to deal with as she pleases. I've nay interest in acquiring that from your daughter or family."

And he meant it. Money was of no interest to him. He had plenty. Culzean and his estates were very successful. His father, grandfather, and the rest of his line before them were all incredibly savvy with running the Kennedy books.

The knowledge that even though he'd only asked for permission to court Lizzie, not marry her, though that was how they were speaking, was not lost on him. He actually quite liked the idea of spending his days with Lizzie.

Could he see her as Lady Kennedy? He could. With her personality she would run his estates with ease and authority.

But he couldn't get ahead of himself. Hell's teeth, he couldn't very well propose yet.

Or could he? It wasn't that long ago that he'd sworn off ever being in a committed relationship. But with Lizzie he also learned that it was okay to trust in someone. To believe in them. Something that, outside of his group of friends, he hadn't done since the war.

"Well, I think cheers are in order." Barclay held up his glass of whisky, pulling Malcolm's attention back to him. "Slàinte Math!"

Malcolm dipped his head in thanks and repeated the cheer. "Slàinte Math!" Then in one long swallow emptied his glass of whisky and set the glass down.

Standing, he held out his hand to shake Barclay's. "I thank ye for your blessing. I vow to take great care of her."

"I shall hold ye to that promise. Now, I'm sure ye want to give the good news to Lizzie. Go on. For certain she is pacing the hall waiting for an answer."

Malcolm nodded and swept out of the room. It didn't take long to find Lizzie, she practically launched herself at him as he rounded the corridor that would lead him to the solar where he expected to find her.

"Well, what did he say?" she asked impatiently, between a smattering of kisses she planted on his cheeks.

He laughed aloud. "'Tis a good thing your papa said aye, otherwise this behavior would be most improper and have ye confined to your room."

She hugged him close. "I kenned he would say aye."

"How so?" he asked as he set her on her feet but kept ahold of her hand.

"He could see it. He's quite observant."

"Aye. So what shall we do now?"

"The hour grows late, but we could catch a show at the theater. If ye like the theater, that is. Funny, I've ne'er asked. I just assumed ye do. But ye may no'. We dinna have to go to—"

"Lizzie, Lass." He grasped her arms and spun her to face him. "Stop. Whate'er makes ye happy, I will do."

So they did. The theater that night was their first foray into society as a couple. Lizzie received some looks that he could only describe as jealousy, but she didn't let them bother her in the least.

Malcolm was unsure what the lasses were jealous of. He'd never seen them before, so surely, he wasn't a potential suitor for them anyhow.

Sitting in the box that Barclay was kind enough to let them use, they watched the play as it unfolded in front of them.

The theater had never been one of his favorite things to do, but with Lizzie at his side, watching her reactions throughout the play, he found he was quite enjoying himself.

But it wasn't the play.

It was his company.

LIZZIE FELT LIKE she was floating as she and Malcolm arrived to watch the play. Women she had kenned for years raised their eyebrows in surprise as Malcolm escorted her to their seat. A couple of them actually approached them to introduce themselves.

Of course, Lizzie kenned what they were doing. Fishing for information, no less. It didn't matter. Their courtship would be all over the gossip papers in the morning.

And she didn't mind that one bit.

"Well, Lizzie, who do we have here?" Matilda Smith asked as she lifted her hand for Malcolm to take.

Lizzie rolled her eyes at the audacity of the woman. They had attended etiquette school together and Matilda always took flirting to a whole new level as she looked at Malcolm, batting her eyelashes while she curtsied low to give him a glimpse of her cleavage.

With a reluctant sigh, she made the introductions. "Malcolm, this is Matilda, an old classmate. Matilda, this is Malcolm Kennedy, Earl of Cassilis."

"Earl," she drawled, dropping into another curtsy. "My lord, 'tis a pleasure to meet ye."

Malcolm dipped his head in acknowledgment.

"What brings ye to Stonehaven?"

Not missing a beat, Malcolm bent and placed a kiss on Lizzie's cheek. "Lizzie brought me here. And happy I am for it."

Matilda's eyes rounded in shock. "Well, that is a surprise. A lucky woman she is," she remarked sarcastically.

"Nay," Malcolm countered, shaking his head. "'Tis I that is lucky." He picked up her hand and kissed the top, letting his lips linger.

Matilda gasped and quickly excused herself.

When she was gone, Lizzie struck him in the chest playfully. "Ye are awful," she said with a giggle.

"Awful, but truthful." His eyes held hers and heat pooled in her stomach. Whenever he looked at her with such intensity, she felt like she could drown in those beautiful eyes of his.

"For certain, Matilda has run off to her circle of friends and is telling them all about us."

"I have no regrets."

With intermission finished, the curtains pulled open, and the second half of the play began. They sat in silence, watching the conclusion unfold in front of them. All the while, Malcolm held her hand and she couldn't stop thinking about how lucky she was.

Earl or nay, Malcolm was a special man, and he'd chosen her. And that made her ridiculously happy.

"Me neither."

Later that night, after she'd retired to her room, she practically felt as if she were floating. So happy was she, she couldn't stop the squeal that burst from her mouth.

When she'd bid Malcolm a good night, he was once again speaking with her papa in the study. They talked of subjects she found most uninteresting—accounts, estates, business. The conversation made Lizzie's eyes glaze over, so she excused herself and let them continue.

A knock sounded and Mary poked her head inside the room.

"Come in!" Lizzie exclaimed excitedly, patting the bed beside her.

"Miss, ye are the talk of the estate. I am no' surprised in the least." She looked towards the closed door. "No' only because of the kisses I saw ye both stealing, but ye and the earl's eyes gave it away e'ery time each of ye looked at each other."

"I can hardly believe Papa agreed."

"Pfft. Why wouldna he? Lord Kennedy is an earl. Ye will be a lady, miss."

Lizzie squealed again. "We have no' discussed marriage, and no proposal has been made. 'Tis just a courtship right now."

"Och, 'tis plain to see. A proposal will most certainly be forthcoming."

Did she even dare to wish for it? She didn't want to hope for something that might not come to fruition, but oh, she wanted it to be so. More than she was willing to admit.

"Let's get ye ready for bed. After your trip to the theater, ye and the earl will be the talk of the city."

She sighed. It had been some time since the Barclay name had been the talk of society. Not since the death of her brother those years ago. At least this time the interest was for good news.

Well, Matilda may say otherwise, but Lizzie paid her no attention. Though they were acquainted through etiquette school, they had never spent any time together outside of that. Matilda held herself in way too high regard for Lizzie's liking.

But none of that mattered.

Matilda's attitude and personality promised that she would grow old alone. Unless her parents married her off. Because right now, Matilda had no prospects, and her countenance guaranteed that none would be forthcoming with the exception of her parents coming into a large sum of money. They were not poor by any means, but Lizzie was sure her dowry was modest at best.

She didn't want to think about Matilda. Instead, her thoughts shifted to Malcolm and a smile broke out on her face. She couldn't help it.

"Ye will be mistress of Culzean Castle, Miss. How exciting is that?"

"Mary! Dinna say such things." Her cheeks heated at the thought. She'd never run a household afore. The mere thought made her break out in a cold sweat. Would she be up to the job? Of course, she'd seen her mother run Tolton Hall like a well-oiled engine. But it was something completely different when she thought of having to do the same thing herself. And for a castle, no less.

"Och, dinna fash about it now, Miss. Ye will have plenty of time for such things in the future when the time arises. For now, ye just need to concentrate on the here and now."

Lizzie dropped back on the bed, sinking into the soft mattress. "I wonder what the morrow will bring. For certain, Malcolm willna leave for Culzean right away." Or would he? She worried her bottom lip.

Mary pulled the drapes shut over the windows, blocking out the moonlit sky.

"I dinna think he will, Miss. I have a feeling that he will be spending a fair amount of time in Stonehaven." She patted the chair in front of the vanity. "Come sit and I'll brush your hair before bed. Ye need your rest for the morrow. I've a feeling 'twill be a busy one and ye want to look your best."

Mary was right. The last thing she wanted when she faced everything tomorrow was her eyes puffy with lack of sleep.

After her hair was brushed to a shine, Mary ordered her under the covers. And as she drifted off to sleep, visions of Malcolm's handsome face flooded her mind. She burrowed into the blankets, a smile on her face. Life couldn't possibly get better than this, she thought before falling asleep.

How very wrong she had been.

CHAPTER SEVENTEEN

"I HOPE THIS room will be to your satisfaction," Barclay said as he pushed open the door to one of Tolton Hall's guest rooms.

Malcolm glanced at the large bed set against the wall in the center of the room and nodded. As long as he had a comfortable bed, he was good. He looked forward to a good night's sleep after the past few nights. "This will be fine. I thank ye for your kindness."

"I shall leave ye to it then. I will see ye in the morn."

Shutting the door, Malcolm walked around the room. Dark-blue wallpaper covered the walls, decorated in swirls of gold foil.

Several framed portraits hung on the walls. He took some time to study each one. An oil painting of Lizzie's parents. One of her grandmama. One of her grandmama with whom he assumed was Lizzie's grandpapa.

There was one of Lizzie as a young lass. She was sitting in a meadow of flowers, a small basket in her pudgy hands, her cherub cheeks aglow with delight. He couldn't help but smile. She looked so happy.

He wondered if their daughter would look like her.

"Jesus, Kennedy," he mumbled to the empty room. He was acting like a lovesick lad. Though the image of Lizzie, belly round with his bairn, awakened a yearning in him that he never kenned existed before.

Children were not something he thought about. Not his own anyway. His friends were quite happy with their wee ones running around, and the tots were adorable. But seeing them hadn't made him want any of his own.

Not until Lizzie. With her, he could picture them. Long for them even. A lass that favored Lizzie's looks. A lad, strong and determined like him.

Malcolm shook his head as he pushed his hands through his hair. This time he'd spent with Lizzie had surely provided him with the excitement he'd been missing. Even if it was of an entirely different kind that he was looking for.

He moved on to the next hanging portrait and his eyes narrowed as a sliver of recognition slid down his spine. Dropping his gaze to the name, he swore as it confirmed his initial thoughts. Angus Barclay.

Angus.

"Fuck," he cursed the empty room as memories from the war flooded his brain. The traitor he'd caught and essentially signed his death warrant was Lizzie's brother.

How the hell could he tell her that? She would never forgive him. Rightly so. It didn't matter that everything her brother had done was against the crown. Against his country. It didn't matter that he kenned the risks and consequences when he decided to sell their plans and secrets to the enemy.

He stumbled back and collapsed into a chair, cradling his head in his hands.

"Shite!" He rammed his fist against the arm of the chair. "What do I do? What do I do?" he murmured to no one.

This was the worst of situations. Lizzie loved her brother. She spoke highly of him whenever she'd mentioned him in their conversations. He understood that he had passed, but not once had she ever spoken about how.

Did she truly ken? Surely at least her parents kenned the reason.

He groaned. How did one of the happiest days of his life turn into one of the worst, reminding him of a time in his life he constantly tried to forget. The betrayal he'd felt when he'd uncovered Angus as the traitor was like a knife to the gut.

Discovering that Angus was Lizzie's brother? That was like a knife to his heart.

He pushed from the chair and paced the floor. The number of times he walked from one side of the room to the other he couldn't say. But he was surprised that he hadn't worn a path in the gray rug.

His mind was too busy running through scenarios of how he could explain to Lizzie how he played a part in her brother's death to be able to sleep.

What a messed-up situation he found himself in. And he wasn't sure he would be able to talk his way out of it.

Lizzie was understanding, but this was different. This was her family. Her only brother.

He hung his head, his hands dropping to his sides. He needed whisky. Lots of it. It's the only thing that would quiet all the noise running through his head.

In his search of whisky, Malcolm made his way quietly downstairs. A feat harder than it needed to be considering he just wanted to stomp his boots down the steps. The estate was dark. It matched his mood as he crept along the quiet halls.

It would be considered an intrusion to enter Barclay's study, even if he kenned that for certain he would find whisky within its walls. Mayhap he would have some luck in the kitchen. He entered the room and found a lit lantern on the countertop and groaned.

At the noise, Lizzie jumped where she stood in front of the stove. "Malcolm. Ye frightened me."

The source of his angst looked at him with tired eyes.

"What are ye doing awake, Lass?"

She pointed to the pot on the flame. "I couldna sleep. Needed my trusty warm milk to help." Her gaze met his, her eyes warm and inviting.

He clenched his jaw, not daring himself to speak.

"Today was quite the whirlwind. I find my excitement of all that's happened is keeping me awake." She turned off the flame and poured the milk into a mug.

Sidling up to him in a way he found way too erotic, she didn't stop until she was flush against his chest.

He closed his eyes. But Lord help him, he couldn't resist this woman. He wrapped his arms around her and pulled her close, kissing the top of her head. Inhaling, he savored the scent of her shampoo. He would miss this scent.

Because surely, on the morrow, when he revealed the truth, she would banish him from Tolton Hall and never want to speak with him again. Never want to see him again.

So he would enjoy this last moment of peace with her, snuggled against his chest, sighing in contentment.

And when she tipped her face up to his, it took all of his strength not to capture her lips in his. He wanted to, though. Lord how he wanted to.

Instead, he placed a soft kiss on her forehead, letting his lips linger for just a moment too long. "Ye better get back to bed, lass. I dinna think your father would be too happy if he found ye down here with me."

She pushed back, creating a small distance between them, and he immediately missed the heat of her.

"Why are ye no' in your room?"

"Pardon?"

"I came down for a cup of warm milk. What is your reasoning?"

"Och. I also couldna sleep."

"Here. Take this." She offered him her mug of milk. "I can warm up more."

He shook his head. "Nay, lass. Ye go on. I fear I'm in search of something stronger."

She studied his face and he felt as if she could see into his very soul.

Read all the thoughts going through his mind.

"Is something amiss?" she asked, her brows creased in concern.

"Nay. All is well," he lied.

The narrowing of her eyes told him that she didn't believe him.

"What arena ye telling me? Malcolm?"

Pressing his lips together, he shook his head. "'Tis naught. Please, Lass," he nearly begged. "Return to your chambers. I will be doing the same as soon as I find what I've come in search of."

"What are ye looking for? Mayhap I can help," she offered. Stubbornly ignoring his plea to go to her room.

"Whisky."

"Hmmm." She tapped her finger on her cheek. "Papa always has some in his study, but I believe Cook uses it as well." She placed her mug on the counter and grabbed the lantern to search the cupboards and shelves. "Aha!" She spun around, whisky bottle in hand. "Here ye go."

He accepted the bottle and dipped his head in thanks. "Now, go back upstairs afore someone sees us."

She grabbed her mug of milk and approached him. Lifting on her toes, she placed her lips on his cheek, and he leaned into the kiss. "Sleep well, Malcolm. I shall see ye in the morn."

He nodded, and watched her disappear out of the room, taking the light of the lantern with her. When he was drowned in darkness, he popped the cap off the bottle of whisky, and most ungentlemanlike, took a swig straight from the bottle.

The night was long. But yet, he almost wished it would last an eternity. Because then he wouldn't have to break the heart of the woman that he loved.

His thought hit him like a punch in the gut.

Love.

It was true. He loved Lizzie Barclay.

But she would never love him back.

>>>><<<<

SOMETHING WAS OFF with Malcolm. His demeanor in the kitchen was... Lizzie couldn't quite put her finger on it, but he was acting funny.

Her heart sank. Mayhap he was having second thoughts about their courtship. Ignoring the mug of warm milk she'd prepared earlier, she collapsed onto the bed.

"Damn it," she cursed, fisting the bed coverings. "Me and my stupid forwardness."

Mama was right. She had repeatedly told her to rein in her personality, and for the most part, she thought she had done a good job of doing so. But when it came to her attraction to Malcolm, the inexplicable pull word him, she found it hard to control herself.

She covered her eyes with her arm and groaned. What had she been thinking? She'd practically demanded that he go to her father and ask permission to court her.

What if Malcolm had done it only to appease her in the moment? A way to rid himself of a wee beastie.

She must talk to him. Apologize for her behavior. If she could put him at ease, mayhap that would change his mind.

Sitting up, decision made, she slipped he feet into slippers and pulled on her robe, cinching it tight around her waist.

Her nerves were on edge, and her heart beat fast as she made her way down the hall to the room Malcolm was staying in.

Knocking on the door quiet enough that she hoped wouldn't wake anyone else, she stepped back and held her breath as she waited for Malcolm to answer.

Moments seemed to stretch on forever. Mayhap he was asleep and hadn't heard.

She knocked again.

The door cracked open, and Malcolm's eyes blew wide at the sight of her. He pulled the door open, and stuck his head out into the hall, looking back and forth.

"Lass, what are ye doing here?" he whispered, then yanked her inside and shut the door.

His honey-colored hair was crazy, the ends standing up straight in every direction. His clothes disheveled. He looked like he'd been through Hell and then dragged back to the land of the living.

Her back against the door, she watched him.

"Ye shouldna be here." He pushed his hands roughly through his hair.

She could smell the whisky on his breath. Her eyes flashed to the near empty bottle. Clearly, something was amiss.

"I couldna sleep," she whispered.

"Isna that what ye got the milk for?"

She nodded. "At first, aye. But once I got back to my room, warm milk couldn't help. What is wrong? And dinna ye dare tell me 'tis naught. I ken ye are lying."

His eyes were sad as he looked at her, but he remained silent.

"If ye dinna want this courtship, please ken that ye can walk away. I willna shackle ye to a life ye dinna want." No matter how much it would break her heart.

"What?" His gaze was incredulous. "Lass, I verra much want this." He approached her, his strong fingers caressing her cheek. "Och, more than ye ken."

"Then, pray tell, what is the issue? What has happened?" she implored, emotion making her voice crack.

He began to pace the floor of the room, scrubbing his hands up and down his face.

She was at a loss trying to understand what was happening. The pain darkening his beautiful blue eyes broke her heart. But she didn't ken how to fix it. Especially when he refused to tell her what it was.

Pushing off the door, she grasped his hands, forcing him to stop his pacing and dragged him to sit upon the bed with her. She felt the heat emanating off his body through the material of her robe. Mayhap sitting beside him was not the best of ideas. Images of him pushing her back onto the soft mattress, covering her body with his, flooded her mind.

Focus, Lizzie, she chided herself.

Palming his face in her hands, she forced him to look at her. His gaze was pure agony.

"What is it? Whate'er 'tis, it canna be as bad as ye think. Talk to me, Malcolm. Please," she begged.

He grasped her wrists, leaned his face into her palms. "If I do, ye will hate me fore'er," he confessed.

She couldn't imagine what he could possibly say that would have such an effect on her feelings for him. "Nay," she said with a shake of her head. "I dinna believe that. Malcolm." She grabbed one of his large hands, enveloping it in hers that seemed so small in comparison. Gingerly, she placed her lips on his warm skin. She kenned the action may seem odd to him, but it felt so natural to her. She wanted to offer him comfort.

To show him that the feelings that filled her heart and mind were true. They weren't the feelings of a child that didn't understand what love was.

She did. The realization washed over her.

She loved him.

She loved Malcolm Kennedy.

"I love ye, Malcolm."

He shook his head violently. "Dinna say such things, Lass. Take it back."

He said it as if it were something that could be so easily done. As if they were just words that held no meaning. But they did. They held deep meaning.

"I willna. And afore we retired for the evening, I would have wagered a bet that ye felt the same. Something has changed. I just dinna ken what."

She pushed off the bed and walked around the room, fidgeting with the tie of her robe.

"I just want ye to talk to me, Malcolm."

"Your brother," he said quietly. "His name was Angus?"

Her brows furrowed and she frowned. What did Angus have to do with any of this? "Aye," she whispered. A pang of sadness piercing her chest at the memory of her brother.

"How did he pass?"

"In the war. I believe we discussed this previously. Malcolm, I'm confused."

She tracked his gaze to her brother's portrait. It was one of her favorites of Angus. He had just turned three and ten and was posing with one of the family dogs, a huge smile on his freckled face.

"Ye did say he died in the war. But do ye ken what happened?"

Pulling her stare from the portrait, her gaze clashed with Malcolm's, his eyes intense. Blinking away tears that were threatening to sprout in her eyes, she nodded. "He died a hero. Tracking close to enemy lines. He was found and executed on the spot. 'Twas awful."

He closed his eyes and blew out a long breath.

"Who told ye that?"

"My parents." She cocked her head to the side and studied him. "Why are ye asking about my brother? What does he have to do with anything? Ye've ne'er e'en met him."

He guffawed, a small laugh escaping his lips as he shook his head.

"That is where ye are wrong. I did ken him. Verra well, as a matter of fact."

"Ye kenned my brother? Why did ye no' say anything? And why is that aught but good?"

Malcolm pinched the bridge of his nose. "I didna realize he was your brother until I saw the portrait and recognized him."

She threw her hands up in exasperation. "I still am missing something. Tell me what 'tis."

CHAPTER EIGHTEEN

T HE BARCLAYS WOULD have received a letter after Angus's execution. Along with a visit from an officer or two, as well.

An investigation would have been conducted to ensure Angus acted alone and the elder Barclays had absolutely no part in his treachery. Since they'd kept their status and estates, naught had come from the inquest, but surely they were aware of what their son had done.

He wrestled with what to tell Lizzie. It was clear that her parents had not informed her of the true account of her brother's death. More than likely to save her impression of the brother she dearly loved.

Malcolm could understand that, but it made his position worse than it was before.

"Did officers visit Tolton Hall after your brother's death?" he asked.

Lizzie sighed. "Of course. I wasna privy to the conversations that were held, obviously. But afterward my parents took me aside and explained what had happened and that Angus wouldna be coming home." She dabbed at the tears that filled her eyes. "I am sorry. I still miss him so."

He nodded. "I understand. I've no siblings myself, but I can only imagine the special bond ye must have shared."

She sniffled and bobbed her head. "'Twas. I am still at a loss as to what his death has to do with whate'er 'tis that's happening."

He blew out a breath. He was at a crossroads. Did he tell Lizzie the truth and lose her forever? Or did he make up some farce of a story, break their courtship, along with her heart, and lose her forever?

Both options ended with him alone and Lizzie's heart broken.

He grabbed the bottle of whisky and took a long pull. He made a mental note to ensure he left payment for the bottle he'd consumed.

No matter what, there was no getting out of this situation with his heart intact.

Lizzie straightened her shoulders and pierced him with a serious gaze. "When I was in my room, thinking about the conversation we'd shared in the kitchen, I was kicking myself for ruining e'erything."

"Nay—"

She held her hand up, stopping him from saying aught else.

"I had thought my forwardness, which Mama always said would get me into trouble, finally did just that. My idea to come in and apologize, to let ye ken that I would rein in my urges to speak afore I think."

"Lass, I would ne'er want ye to change." He approached her and put his hands on her shoulders. "Ye are strong. Ye're fierce. Dinna e'er change that. For anyone."

She laughed and stepped from his touch.

"That was my original thought. That 'twas me. Something I had done. But all of this talk of my brother has led me to believe that 'tis something else." She sat in the chair set by the small fireplace and met his eyes. "There's obviously something about my brother's death that I am unaware of. And apparently ye do. So, tell me what I am missing. Now."

Her strong countenance was commendable. But he was still torn on what he should do. It really should be her parents to tell her. He didn't want to see the look of disdain when she learned that he was the reason for her brother's death.

How could she ever love him after finding such a thing out? It didn't matter that Angus was a traitor. That he was working against the crown. That wasn't the brother she kenned. The brother she remembered was kind and loving. Someone she had grown up with. An innocent boy.

But he wasn't. Far from it. But he still couldn't tell her.

"'Tis no' for me to say, Lass. I believe that is a conversation to be had betwixt ye and your parents. Ye need to return to your room. The hour is late, and your father would have my head if he found ye in here with me—in your nightclothes, no less."

"Ye arena going to tell me?" She crossed her arms in front of her chest, her hip jutted out to the right.

If the situation were different, he would find her stance most attractive. But right now, it just broke his heart. He needed her to leave his room. To return to her own.

He just shook his head. Not trusting his voice to say anything.

For a few long moments, she stood there, glaring at him, searching his face for answers that he wouldn't give her.

He just hung his head in defeat.

Finally, she took a deep breath and jutted her chin out defiantly. "I bid ye a good night, Malcolm."

And with that, she spun around and left the room.

When she was gone, the space felt lonely. Her presence was so big that she sucked the life out of the room when she left.

Exhaling in exasperation, he picked up the whisky bottle and finished it in one long swallow, hissing at the burn as it wound his way down his throat and settled warmly into his chest.

In the morn, when Lizzie woke, he would be gone. On his way back to Culzean. If her parents wanted to tell her the truth of her brother's death, so be it. But 'twouldna be him.

He was being evasive. He kenned it. Instead of facing the woman he loved and the hurt that she would surely feel, he was running.

Like a cat with its tail tucked between its legs. A coward.

Something he had never been labeled afore.

But he was now. He was admitting to himself that that's exactly what he was.

He threw his clothes into his travel bag. And after some time, when he was sure the house was quiet and no one would see him leave, he slipped out of his room and out the front door.

In the stables, he readied a horse and gave the stableboy a note to cover the cost of the horse and whisky, along with a missive that he was to deliver to Sir Barclay in the morning.

Then he was gone, riding through the gates of Tolton Hall, not daring to look back. He'd push the steed as far as he could until he had to stop and give them both a rest. But he wanted to make it back to Culzean as quickly as possible.

For once, he looked forward to the monotony of his well-run, issue-free home.

AFTER TOSSING AND turning all night, dawn couldn't come soon enough. Lizzie was awake and sitting in the window seat of her bedroom when Mary knocked to wake her.

"Ah, Miss, ye're already awake? Could ye no' sleep last night?"

Lizzie shook her head. "E'en a mug of warm milk couldna help," she admitted quietly.

"Are ye no' feeling well? If ye're ill I shall call for the doctor." Mary turned to leave and Lizzie called her back.

"'Tis no' that. I just had a worrisome night thinking of the earl."

Mary waggled her eyebrows. "Worrisome or dreamlike?" She smiled, but when Lizzie didn't laugh, her lips dipped into frown.

"Ye went to bed so happy. What has happened? I dinna believe the earl has left his room yet this morn. His door remains shut."

Lizzie didn't ken what to tell her friend. She didn't even ken what to tell herself. This morn her mind was still confused. Playing their conversation over and over again. It just kept leading to her brother. But whatever it was, Malcolm wouldn't say.

She'd decided that she would confront her parents about it when they all gathered to break their fast. Malcolm would be there as well and certainly he wouldn't dare tell her not to broach the subject with her parents.

They didn't oft talk about Angus. Once he'd passed, they'd stayed mum about discussing him. She had found that odd but decided that was how they grieved. Everyone did so in their own way. Whereas Lizzie would rather talk about the fun times they'd shared, her parents always had her cease the conversation when she started it.

Today she would find out why.

The truth this time.

When she arrived in the dining room to break her fast, the first thing Lizzie noticed was that Malcolm was not in the room. The next thing she noticed was the dour moods of her parents. She took her seat and waited for her tea to be poured and the room empty before asking her parents what was going on.

First Malcolm, and now them. Obviously, things were running afoul and she was the only one that wasn't privy to the issues. It irritated her more than she wanted to admit. Usually, she didn't concern herself with issues her parents faced. Selfish, she kenned. However, they had always purposely sheltered her from such things, so that now it was normal for her to just leave the room when such serious conversations began.

Today was different. It appeared that the issues going on, whatever they were, involved her. And she refused to ignore it.

"I would verra much like to wish you both a good morn, but the sour looks on your faces would indicate otherwise. Has something happened?"

"Lizzie." It was her mother that addressed her. "Some things have come to light that we need to discuss."

"Will Malcolm be joining us to break his fast?" she asked hopefully. Praying that last night was just a bad night. That mayhap he'd eaten something that didn't settle well with him. But deep down, she kenned that wasn't the case.

"He willna," her father said quietly. There was a somber tone to his voice and it immediately filled her with worry.

"Does he fare well?" Mayhap he had an accident. He was definitely in his cups when she'd left his room last night.

"He is fine. At least, I think so."

She raised a brow in question, utterly confused.

"Dearest." It was her mother speaking to her again. "Your father and I have something to discuss with ye. Something we should have discussed long ago."

She set down the piece of toast she'd just begun to slather with butter and frowned. "Ye both are acting so odd, ye have me worried."

Her father spoke as her mother wrung her hands together.

"This is a difficult conversation to have with ye. Chances are ye will be upset with us when all is said and done. But we would both like to stress that everything we have done, all of our actions, we felt we did them for your benefit."

"Well, now ye have me positively scared to hear what ye are going to say," she confessed.

"We ne'er meant to hurt ye. Please believe that."

She took a sip of tea, her hands shaking and causing the liquid to slosh over the rim and onto the saucer.

Clearing his throat, her father continued. "When your brother passed, we were devastated."

Why were they bringing up her brother's death? First Malcolm and now them.

"Rightly so. We all were. He was a good man. At least we could take solace in kenning he died a hero."

At the head of the table, her father stiffened. Beside him, her mother visibly paled.

"About that. Your brother didna die a hero. He, he betrayed the crown. Became a traitor to the country."

And that was how she learned that everything she had believed the past few years was all a lie. It explained why her parents never spoke about him. She remembered early conversations and whispers of how he was a lost soul, misinformed even.

But that couldn't explain away all of the vile things he'd done. Sold secrets to the enemy. Under the excuse of setting up his family's financial future. In doing so, not only did it cost him his life, but it put them all under great scrutiny.

Her parents investigated for possible collusion.

She had no idea how close they'd come to losing their coffers. Their home.

The only home she'd ever kenned.

All because of her brother's selfish and misguided actions. Her dear, sweet brother that she only remembered as kind-hearted and loving. She had a most difficult time seeing him as anything but.

But then the worst news came. Malcolm, the man who held her heart, was the man who had caught Angus red-handed. He'd been assigned by Wellington to uncover the traitor. He'd been doing his job, and in turn, that led to the execution of her brother.

Sobs wracked from her body. Big chest-heaving sobs.

At the loss of her brother. The lies she'd been told. Malcolm's betrayal.

Was it betrayal though? Nay. That's why he acted so funny last night. Her brother's portrait hung in the room he'd been given. He'd obviously recognized him. It wasn't a surprise that he hadn't put he and Lizzie together as siblings. Why would he? There were plenty of Barclays around. It was a very common surname.

"Where's Malcolm now?" she asked, concern creasing her brow as her throat felt like it was closing up.

Her father shook his head. "I dinna ken. He left in the early hours of the morn. More than likely to return home to Culzean."

Nay!

"Why? Why would he do that?"

Did he think she would hold contempt for him? Did she? As much as she wanted to, she couldn't hold Malcolm at fault for doing his job.

Her brother had a job to do as well. And he didn't do it. As much as she loved her brother, she could not condone his actions. They were wrong, and he paid the ultimate price. Just the same as anyone else had they been caught doing such things.

That didn't make Malcolm a horrible person. It made him strong. Loyal.

"We must go to Culzean, then."

"Lizzie," her mother said. "We think it best that we stay here. Give ye time to ponder about all ye've learned."

And that was when the anger hit her. It wasn't anger at Malcolm. Nay, rather her ire was aimed at her parents.

"None of this would have happened if ye'd just told me the truth from the start. Why would ye keep such information from me?"

"'Twas for your benefit." Papa stood and placed his hands on her shoulders, but she shrugged them off.

"Nay," she shook her head. "Ye dinna get to tell me what is best for me. Ye dinna get to make those decisions. I am a grown woman. I am no' a wee lass who doesn't understand the world in which we live. The cruelty of it." She pushed back from the table, her appetite suddenly lost. "I will be in my room."

She ran from the dining hall, swiping at the tears that fell like raindrops in a spring sky. How could her parents not have enough trust in her to think she wouldn't be able to handle the truth?

That betrayal hurt almost as bad as finding out the truth about Angus.

But above everything, she wouldn't, couldn't, hold Malcolm accountable. Out of everyone at play in this whole charade, he was the least culpable.

CHAPTER NINETEEN

A LOUD POUNDING on Malcolm's bedchamber door made him growl out in frustration. "Go away!"

Instead of going away as he'd ordered, the door burst open. "Fuck," he cursed as he covered his eyes from the intrusion of light filtering around the figures in the hallway. He'd been blissfully enjoying the darkness for, well, he couldn't remember for how long, but it had been some time.

"It stinks of whisky and sweat in here."

It was Gunn. He hadn't seen him since the party where he'd first met Lizzie.

Lizzie.

Ignoring his friend, he grasped the bottle and emptied it, then set it on the table to join the others he'd drained.

"Hell's teeth, brother," Alexander, Duke of Argyll, commented as he stepped into the room. "'Tis like a sty in here. Have ye decided to live with the hogs?"

Malcolm didn't answer. Just reached for another bottle of whisky and uncorked the bottle.

"I shall be taking that," Finlay, Earl of Rosebery, stated, snatching the bottle out of his hand.

For once, he wasn't happy to see his friends.

"Give that back." He moved to stand, and the room spun so he flopped back into the chair.

"We kenned ye were bad, but we didna ken 'twas this bad." Alexander waved his hand in the air. "When is the last time ye changed your clothes? Or bathed?"

"Dinna ye all have wives to tend to?" Malcolm mumbled, ignoring his friend's questions. "Is Nicholas going to be walking in the door as well? What are ye all doing here?"

Finlay moved to the windows and pushed the drapes open.

"Damn it," Malcolm swore before covering his eyes. He hadn't seen the light of day since he arrived back to Culzean almost three weeks ago. The brightness burned his eyes causing his head to ache even more.

Or mayhap that was due to the amount of whisky he'd been drinking. He'd lost track at how many bottles he was up to.

"Shut the damn curtains," he ordered to no avail.

"No' a chance. And nay, Nicholas is staying home. Gwen is round with their next bairn that is due any day now."

He should be happy for his friend. Happy that he would be blessed with another baby, but all he could think about was what he'd lost with Lizzie. How he'd never get the chance to see her belly round with their own bairn.

The realization of that was like a knife to the gut.

"Ye need to get out of this room, brother. Ye are doing yourself nay favors hiding away." Gunn stood in front of him, arms crossed, his forehead creased with concern.

"I am nay good to anyone anyway."

"Bollocks," Alexander snapped. "Are ye giving up? Just like that. You're not e'en going to put up a fight? That's no' the Malcolm Kennedy I ken."

"Ye dinna understand."

Finlay stretched his arms out. "Then tell us. We are all ears."

"I killed her brother."

"What?" Alexander asked. "Who?"

"Lizzie's brother. Angus."

Finlay cocked his head to the side, deep in thought. "Angus." His eyes lit up with awareness. "The traitor?"

"The verra one."

"Let's be honest. The only one that got Angus killed was himself. He kenned the risks and still did the crime."

"Aye." He waved his hand in the air. "I ken all that. But all Lizzie sees is that I killed her brother. She had nay idea he had e'en been executed. She thought he'd died a hero."

"What?"

He squeezed his eyes shut. Lord, his head hurt. "Aye, her parents lied to her about his death to preserve her happy memories of him."

"But now she kens the truth, aye?" Gunn asked.

Malcolm shrugged. He hadn't stuck around long enough to see how they handled the situation. For all he kenned, she still thought Angus was a hero.

"So certainly she understands that 'tis no' ye that killed him," Gunn pressed. When Malcolm remained silent, he pushed. "Well?"

Malcolm shrugged. "I dinna ken."

"What do ye mean?"

"I left. I didn't want to break her heart. Or face the contempt on her face when she learned the truth."

"Ye ran?" Alexander asked incredulously.

As he should. Malcolm had never run from anything. Ever.

Until now.

He could only nod.

"Are ye daft? What were ye thinking?"

He leaned forward and cradled his head in his hands. "I was thinking that I was saving her heart. Because clearly, I broke it by condemning her brother to death."

Finlay left the room. He was probably disappointed in the man Malcolm had become and couldn't stand to look upon him anymore.

He couldn't blame him. He couldn't stand himself either.

"So, to save her heart, ye broke yours? Without kenning if ye would have lost her in the first place." Alexander shook his head. "If Clarissa were here," he said, referring to his wife, "she'd box your ears for your stupidity."

"Ye love her?" Gunn asked.

If Malcolm was alone he would have probably cried. Aye, he loved her. So verra much. "With all my heart. I canna see my life without her."

"That's all we needed to ken."

"What?"

"All set in here," Finlay called from somewhere down the hall.

"Brother," Gunn uttered as he approached and yanked him to his unsteady feet, "'tis time to get yourself together."

Alexander grabbed his other arm and they hauled him out the door and down the hall. Into the bathing room where the tub had been filled with hot, steaming water.

"Ye need to sober up and clean up. And then get your mind out of whatever stupor it's in and go get your woman."

"She doesna want me."

"That's bullshite, and ye ken it."

When he didn't make a move to undress, his friend stepped forward and started the process.

"Hey, hey!" Malcolm called out. "Cease!"

"Then do it yourself or I swear I will strip you to your bare arse and throw ye in the tub myself," Gunn warned.

Malcolm had no doubt he could. His friend was huge. Broad as a barn. He owned an inn and a pub, and he himself saw to it that no trouble ever broke out.

"Fine. Get out," he grumbled, tugging off his shirt.

"We'll wait for ye in your study."

And that's where they were once he'd finished bathing and dressing in a clean set of clothes. He did feel better, but he wasn't about to admit it to his friends.

"Well, well, well," Alexander quipped, sniffing the air. "Look who no longer appears to be on the verge of death and no longer reeks like a distillery."

"Have ye cleared your head?" Finlay asked.

His head pounded as if it were being constantly struck by a rock, but his thoughts were clear. He nodded.

"So, what's your plan? Are ye going to stay here feeling sorry for yourself or are ye going to go to your lady?"

His friends were right. Could Lizzie blame him? Possibly. But he would never ken unless he confronted her. Could she turn him away and tell him that she never wanted to lay eyes upon him again?

She could. And it would shatter his already broken heart, but at least he would ken the truth. Her true feelings.

He wouldn't be left wondering if he'd missed the opportunity to spend the rest of his life with the woman of his dreams.

"I need my horse," he announced.

"Atta boy," Alexander pounded him on his back. "We kenned ye'd come around."

"And he's saddled up and waiting for ye," Finlay said with a smile.

"Go get her, brother. It will all work out in the end." Gunn smacked him on the back.

"Thank ye," Malcolm said quietly, heading toward the door. "If ye hadn't pushed me, I'd still be drowning my sorrows. I may still once I talk to Lizzie. But at least I will ken for certain the reason why."

With that, he slipped out the door, his friends hooting and hollering as they cheered him on. Their loud yells made his head hurt even more, but he didn't care. As always, his friends had come through for him. Giving him the push that he kenned he needed to take but hadn't dared.

He only hoped and prayed he wasn't too late.

And that Lizzie wouldn't turn him away.

"I NEED TO see him, Mary," Lizzie groaned as she lay on her bed staring at the ceiling. The same thing she'd done almost every day since Malcolm had left.

He had taken over her mind, her thoughts. Every waking moment she thought about him. Every sleeping moment she dreamed about him.

"Miss," Lizzie warned, "your parents willna allow it. Not after the last time that started this whole mess in the first place."

"Do ye think he loves me?" she asked, changing the subject. She didn't ken why she asked Mary the question. She already kenned the answer, but it was as if she were searching for validation from someone other than herself. She certainly couldn't go to her parents and ask such a question.

Mary looked at her, sympathy shining in her eyes. "I cannot speak for the earl, Miss. But he seemed verra taken with ye before," she paused searching for the right words, "before e'erything came to light.

Relations between them had been filled with tension after she'd found out the truth about Angus. She couldn't believe they'd lied to her all this time. She felt like a fool. And she was still angry with them. It would have been so much easier if they'd told her what really happened surrounding his death.

Their lies forced Malcolm to leave. Above all else, that was what really angered her.

They'd made her lose the one thing that held her heart.

Her now shattered heart.

She wanted to put the pieces back together and the only way she could do that would be to see Malcolm. She had to ask him if he loved her. She sighed. She kenned he did, but she wanted to hear the words from his beautiful, full lips. And then she wanted to feel his strong arms wrap her in an embrace as he whispered to her that he was never going to leave her again.

Probably the dreams and whims of a young lass.

But the only way to find out was to ask him. She needed to find a way to go to him.

She sat up, bringing her knees up to her chest and rested her chin on them as she thought.

"Rosalyn lives no' far from here," she stated suddenly.

"Your friend from years ago?"

Lizzie nodded her head. "Aye. She's near, but no' too near. I could tell Mama and Papa that I need to clear my head. Get out of the house and talk to someone near my age that may understand what I'm going through. Surely, they'll agree."

"Miss, I am no' certain that is the best of ideas. Does she still live there with her parents?"

"I believe so, I havena heard that she's married and moved away."

"Do ye think she will see ye?"

Lizzie laughed. "Mary, sometimes ye are so silly. I have no intentions of actually going to visit her. I will use that as an excuse to get us out of the house. Once out, we will make our way to Culzean."

"Nay, absolutely no'." Mary shook her head vehemently. "One time was enough. I nearly lost my job, if ye recall."

Lizzie rolled her eyes. "Ye didna. I would no' allow that to happen, and ye ken it. From the get go, I told my parents that ye were only doing what I told ye to do. The same will apply here."

"I canna condone such a plan, Miss."

"Ye dinna have to, Mary." She pushed off the bed and walked over to her wardrobe, swinging the doors open wide. "Now, come help me pick a few appropriate outfits so that we can be on our way as soon as I convince my parents that I need to talk to someone my own age."

It was Mary's turn to roll her eyes. "Ye are stubborn, Miss." But she joined Lizzie at the wardrobe, and in no time, her travel bag was packed.

Downstairs, she found papa reading his Paper and Mama putting the final touches on her current needlepoint project. They both looked up when she entered the room, and it was as if all the warmth had suddenly been sucked out of the room.

"Mama, Papa," she announced, "I would like to visit Rosalyn for a few days."

Her parents exchanged a look. One that told Lizzie they kenned that she was about to feed them a story.

No matter. She ignored their look and plodded on. "The house is too stuffy. I have all these thoughts running through my head. All these feelings, that quite frankly, I am still confused about. I think it would do me well to be around a peer that can understand what I am going through. Certainly, ye can agree?"

For some odd reason, her mother's mouth turned up into a slight smile, before sharing a knowing look with her father, who nodded his head.

"How long will ye be gone. Or do ye expect to be gone?" Mama asked.

Lizzie was taken aback. Was she not going to have to fight to get them to let her out of the house? This was a most welcome turn of events.

"I hadna thought of the amount of time needed to clear my head. But I think I would need," she quickly calculated how quickly she could make the trip to Edinburgh and back if she pushed, "a week, at least."

"Well, that certainly is a lot of time to catch up with an old friend and to discuss whatever else ye need to. I am sure Rosalyn and her family will be happy to see ye."

"Thank ye." It was all she could think to say after not having to fight for it.

"Ye will be taking Mary?"

"Aye, of course."

"Verra well. We will have the phaeton readied for ye."

"Really?" Now she was beyond flabbergasted. Mayhap they had grown tired of her dourness and just wanted her out of the house for a reprieve. She could understand that.

"Aye, we canna have ye traipsing through the countryside alone on a horse with Mary. Take the carriage and a coachman so you'll be comfortable on the journey."

Her parents were being far too gracious. But, in doing so they were allowing her to make her way to Edinburgh without so much as a fight. She wasn't going to complain or push back.

After securing her travel bag to the back of the phaeton, she turned to her parents, who had come outside to see her off.

"I understand that I have been in a sour mood these past few weeks. I apologize for that. My heart was broken, then broken again, and is still broken. I hope to return with naught but happiness."

Mama pursed her lips and nodded, then gave Lizzie a warm hug. "Be careful," she whispered in her ear.

"The journey to Rosalyn's isna far, Mama. All will be well."

She climbed into the carriage, Mary following closely behind. Once the door was shut and the coachman climbed into his spot, snapping the reins for the horses to start the journey, she looked through the window and gave her parents a wave.

They waved back, smiling warmly.

Again, she found their behavior odd. Were they really that happy to see her go?

Once they were well and good out of sight and earshot from Tolton Hall, Lizzie knocked on the wall of the carriage to alert the driver.

"Aye, Miss?"

"Change of plans," she called out. "We shall travel to Culzean Castle. Make haste, please."

"Aye, Miss." And she heard the snap of the reins and the neigh of the horses as they began to trot.

She narrowed her eyes, somehow, this all seemed too easy. Too convenient.

"What is wrong, Miss?"

"Did Mama and Papa seem a wee bit too eager to see me gone? And why the offer of the carriage? The ride to Rosalyn's isna far." She pointed to the front of the carriage. "And no fight from him about the change in destination? It all strikes me as odd."

"I dinna ken, Miss. Mayhap, they are just eager to see ye happy again?"

Lizzie wasn't sure if that was their reasoning, but she sat back and watched the trees pass through the window. She wouldn't complain about their offer of comfort on this journey.

She remained quiet. Her mind running through all of the things she would say to Malcolm when she saw him.

There was always the possibility he would turn her away. That she would arrive on the steps of Culzean and he wouldn't let her in the door.

She prayed that he would agree to see her.

He had to.

She needed to tell him that she loved him.

If he refused?

Well, she wouldn't accept that as an option.

MALCOLM HAD BEEN riding for two days straight. He was exhausted, bone-weary. His poor horse even moreso.

He'd only stopped in short bursts to allow the horse to rest and drink. He'd feed him an oatcake and then after a brief respite, they'd be back on their way.

He was so close to Tolton Hall. Less than a day's ride now, but his horse needed caring. And as the inn that he'd spent the night with

Lizzie in what seemed forever ago came into view, he kenned he had to stop.

As anxious as he was to see her, he didn't want to arrive on her doorstep smelling of sweat and horse, with the dirt of the road upon his clothes. Nay, he wanted to appear fresh and clean, so he could wrap his arms around her and feel her bury her face into his chest.

He closed his eyes, seeing the scene play out in his mind. It was all he wanted. Mayhap a boyhood fantasy, but he'd had a lot of time to think on this journey.

The love that he felt for Lizzie was true. Now that the pounding ache in his head had ceased, he had thought about how he would explain his actions. Actions regarding her brother. His leaving in the early hours of the morn.

He worried that she felt he'd abandoned her. That wasn't his intention, but he could see how his actions could have been construed as such.

The inn loomed ahead, and he clicked his tongue to get his horse to slow to a stop. A lad grabbed the reins as he hopped off and Malcolm placed a shilling in his hand. "We've had a long journey. He needs food, water, rest, and a good brushing. Care for him well." He untied his travel bag and threw it over his shoulder.

"Aye, my lord," the lad answered as he led the horse around the back. "I will see to him personally."

Malcolm paused in front of the door, looking up at the facade of the inn. Remembering when he was here last.

Soon. Soon, he would see her again. It had been weeks, one more night wouldn't make a difference. That's what he kept telling himself when all he wanted to do was push forward.

Inside, the innkeeper's face broke out into a smile of recognition. "My lord, welcome back. Are ye here for a meal or do ye need a room as well."

"A room, please. Along with a hot bath." He almost asked for a bottle of whisky, but then thought better of it. He wanted his head to remain clear. And ache-less.

"Certainly, follow me."

An hour later, he was soaking his sore muscles in steaming water scented with rosemary. He sighed. The hot water felt amazing, and he could feel his tense muscles relaxing under the heat. The only thing that would make this better was to have Lizzie soaking in the tub with him.

Her naked skin pressed up against his. He groaned. He'd wash her hair, massaging her scalp as he worked his fingers through her long tresses.

He'd wash every inch of her body, running the cloth along her smooth skin. Another groan and his cock jumped to life, standing at attention in the water.

Fighting the urge to fist his length and grant him the relief he so desperately needed, he stepped out of the bath and dried off with the towel that had been hung over the back of the chair.

The bed in the room looked too large and lonely for him to share by himself. An image of Lizzie laying there, her dark hair splayed in contrast to the white sheets, as she looked up at him longingly.

"Shite," he cursed to the empty room, pushing his hands through his damp hair.

He really was obsessed.

Thoughts about his arrival at Tolton Hall entered his mind. Would the Barclays even allow him entry? He hoped, dared to think so.

But he didn't want to just to be allowed entry. Nay, he needed to speak with Lizzie. And if she would have him, he would propose.

Because these past few weeks had been the most insufferable weeks he'd ever had to endure. Worse than the war.

He'd felt like his heart had been ripped out of his chest and he needed the feeling to stop.

His only salvation would be if Lizzie forgave him and accepted his hand in marriage. Only then would the world be put back to rights.

Sitting down at the small desk set near the window, he reached for the ink and paper he'd called for earlier.

Lizzie was one thing. The Barclays were another.

He could only hope his words of solace and apology would be enough for them to accept him and allow him to wed their daughter—if she was willing, of course.

Folding and sealing the letter, he addressed it to the Barclays and brought it downstairs to the innkeeper, who assured him that it would be delivered expeditiously.

"Will ye have guests joining ye for dinner at your table, my lord?"

He shook his head. "I willnae. I must sadly admit, this journey is one I am making alone. But I do hope that the return journey will be different."

"Och, best wishes to ye, my lord," the innkeeper said excitedly. "Dinner will be served within the hour. If ye would like to wait in the salon, there are libations for all tastes there."

Not wanting to go back and face the empty room, he made his way to the salon, but denied any offering of drink. He didn't care to repeat the indulgences of the past few weeks and he wanted to ensure that he kept his head clear for his meeting with Lizzie. Instead, he picked up one of the papers piled on a corner table and read of the local news while he waited.

There wasn't much of interest. A new estate was being built. A barn had burned down. Sadly, the owners had lost a hog. Incredibly, another Phantom Prowler burglary. He couldn't help but smile, kenning who it truly was now, thanks to Lizzie.

A bell chimed making him aware that dinner would soon be served. Folding the paper, he placed it back on the stack and made his way to the dining hall.

"Malcolm?"

He heard his name being called, the voice soft with a tinge of disbelief. But he kenned that voice. Had longed to hear it for weeks. Could it be?

He spun around, and standing in front of him was the most beautiful visage he could ever imagine.

Lizzie.

It all happened so fast. One moment she was standing there, and the next she was running towards his opened arms.

He scooped her up, burying his nose in her lavender-scented hair, and his body roared to life as his heart mended itself back together.

She cried as she clung to his neck, placing kisses on his cheek as she wrapped her legs around him. Having not a care in the world of who was watching.

"What are ye doing here, Lass?"

"I should ask the same of ye."

He set her down and looked around them. Thankfully, the place was empty save for Mary who hung back silently.

"I was coming back to find ye. To explain—"

"Ye dinna need to explain." She clasped his hand and held it tightly. "I understand."

Two simple words, but they meant so much to him. Hope bloomed anew in his chest. Mayhap this would all work out. Just as his friends insisted.

Remembering his manners after being so stunned at seeing her, he asked, "Have ye eaten?"

She shook her head.

"Join me for dinner?"

"I would love that." She accepted his arm and blessed him with the most beautiful smile.

MALCOLM LOOKED SO nervous as he pulled out the chair at the table to allow Lizzie to sit. She would have sworn she saw his hands shaking.

They waited until wine had been poured into each of their glasses and the meal had been served to speak.

She was telling the truth when she'd answered that she hadn't eaten, but she had no appetite. Not for food anyway.

Watching the server walk away, Lizzie sipped her wine, trying to remember all the things she had said she would ask him when she saw him, but her mind drew a blank.

"I canna believe ye are sitting in front of me," she finally said, her voice laced with disbelief. "What are the odds that we stopped at the same inn at the same time?"

"Apparently one hundred percent," he answered, a smile lifting the corners of his mouth.

She giggled. "I suppose ye are right. I say it must be fate."

"I am no' so sure I believe in fate." He took a small sip of wine and she watched as his Adam's apple bobbed up and down in the most fascinating way.

"If no' fate, then what?" she asked, curious of his answer.

"I dinna ken. Luck, which I guess one could chock up to fate. I just ken that I willed this meeting. I played it o'er and o'er again in my mind. I didna ken where. Or when. But I kenned 'twould happen."

He reached over and gently held her hand, his thumb idly caressing her fingers.

Frissons ran up her arm, causing her to shiver.

His brows creased in concern. "Are ye chilled?" He moved to get up. No doubt to find her something to guard against the chill.

"Nay, I am fine, thank ye. I must confess that I also wished for us to meet. I thought 'twould be at Culzean, though."

"Ye were traveling to Culzean?" he asked, eyebrows raised in surprise.

She nodded.

"Alone?"

"Nay, Mary is with me." She stated, confused as she knew he had seen her maid earlier.

Narrowing his eyes, he searched her face. "Isna that how we first met? Ye traveling alone with just your maid? Wait. Do your parents ken ye are traveling?"

"Aye."

Relief washed over him.

"And nay."

His shoulders collapsed and he hung his head for a moment before meeting her gaze again. "Lass, will ye ne'er learn? 'Tis dangerous for ye to travel alone."

"Mama and Papa believe I am visiting a friend nearby. Howe'er, out of character for them, they offered the phaeton and a coachman for the trip."

"For your safety?"

She shrugged. "Mayhap. Things have been," she paused, searching for the right words, "things have been strained since, well, ye ken."

"Lass." He squeezed her fingers, as if trying to send all of his emotions through his hand to her. "I—"

Shaking her head, she pulled her hand back, and tucked a loose wisp of hair behind her ear, then folded her hands on her lap.

"The tension at Tolton Hall has naught to do with ye."

He didn't look convinced as he opened his mouth to say something.

"Dinna speak, please. Let me say what I have to say."

She could see the muscle in his jaw clench, but he remained silent, nodding for her to continue. That he listened and granted her what she asked, meant so much to her. It showed that he respected her.

"When I woke up that morning, I went downstairs to break my fast, expecting ye to be there along with Mama and Papa. I was determined to get to the bottom of whate'er 'twas that ye had alluded to the night before. When ye werena there, I just figured ye were sleeping in.

"Papa told me to have a seat, and that's when I learned the truth about Angus."

A pained look crossed his face and she hurried to reassure him.

"I dinna blame ye, Malcolm. I need ye to understand that. The tension at home was my fault, but 'twas because I was angry at my parents. I was so verra angry that they had lied to me all those years. It explained why they'd ne'er spoken about my brother after his death. They told me he'd died a hero, and then no other conversations were e'er had. Any time I tried to initiate one, they dodged the subject." She paused and took a long swallow of wine.

"'Twas kind of them to try to protect the memories I had of Angus, but I felt like a fool. Walking around all these years thinking he was the bravest man. When he was in fact the opposite. So, nay, I dinna blame ye for the cause of his death. He brought that all on himself. He kenned the risks, and yet he still moved forward with whate'er reprehensible plan he had formed in his mind."

"'Twas still your brother," he said quietly, his voice solemn and laced with guilt.

Guilt that he shouldn't feel.

"He was. But whoe'er he became during the war," she shook her head, "that person wasna my brother. I will fore'er cherish the memories we made when we were younger. But my memories stop when he left for the war. I refuse to think of him as the traitor I now ken he became."

"Ye are verra strong, Lass."

She laughed, twirling the stem of her wine glass. "I dinna ken about that. If I were strong, I would be able to deal with his betrayal. But I canna."

"'Twill take time."

"Mayhap. But what I do ken is ye." She reached out to him and he grasped her hand, his fingers once again caressing her skin. "Ye were doing naught but your job. And from what I was told, 'twas a job ye excelled at. Your name is kenned amongst the highest rankings of officers." She swore she could see a bit of pink color his cheeks at the compliment.

"I did what I had to do for my crown and country. I completed my missions as assigned. I am just so verra sorry that 'twas your brother. He was the last person I expected to catch that fateful night. Until then I had thought he was loyal to me and my unit."

Malcolm's eyes were so serious. She kenned he was speaking from his heart, and she appreciated the truth in his words.

"I can only hope that ye take such good care of me," she said quietly, meeting his gaze with a seriousness of her own.

He searched her face. She watched the emotions play across his as he pondered her words, then watched as his eyes lit up as awareness dawned.

"Are ye saying…" He let the words trail off.

She wasn't sure if it was because he was scared to voice them aloud, but she was sure of what she wanted. Placing her other hand on their clasped ones, she squeezed.

"What I am saying Malcolm Kennedy, Earl of Cassilis, is that I believe ye should marry me."

CHAPTER TWENTY

I T WAS THE most unconventional proposal that Malcolm had ever heard, but it was also the most endearing and sincere.

"Are ye asking me to marry ye, Lass?" He lifted a brow in question.

She tilted her head to the side, the most beautiful smile on her face. "Indeed I am."

"Well, in that case, Annabel Elizabeth Barclay, indeed I will."

Before he could comprehend what she was doing, she launched herself from her chair and closed her arms around his neck. The clatter of dishes captured everyone's attention, and they all stared at them, as he wrapped his arms around her waist and settled her in his lap.

He didn't care. They could stare all they want. Including when he bent and captured her mouth in a searing kiss.

She matched his energy and when he licked the seam of her lips, she opened her mouth, allowing him entry. Their tongues danced together wickedly, and he groaned into her mouth. He heard the low murmur of people in the room, but no amount of talk about impropriety would take away from this moment he and Lizzie were sharing.

"I canna wait to make ye Lady Cassilis," he murmured against her neck.

She giggled in response, also ignoring those around them.

"Lord Kennedy," the innkeeper appeared at the table. "Pardon for the intrusion, but I couldna help but hear the news. Congratulations on your engagement." A server approached the table with a tray and the innkeeper picked up the bottle atop it. "A bottle of our verra best champagne for ye both to celebrate."

Malcolm smiled warmly and bowed his head. "Thank ye. 'Tis most kind of ye to do so."

"May I?" The man pointed to the bottle and Malcolm nodded. "Please."

With that, he uncorked the bottle with a pop, and now that the room understood what was happening, everyone cheered.

He kissed her cheek, which was warm under his lips. "I love ye, lass."

"And I ye, Malcolm. I think I've loved ye since I first saw ye at the Wilsons' party."

They accepted the glasses of champagne that the innkeeper passed to them, and with a cheer to their future, they sipped the bubbly liquid, laughing as the bubbles tickled their noses.

Later, as he escorted Lizzie to her room, he paused, his hands on her waist, not wanting to let her go.

"Now that I've got ye, I dinna want to take my hands off ye," he confessed.

She tipped her head up to his, her brown eyes clashing with his. "Then dinna," she whispered, lifting on her toes and nipping at his lower lip.

The sensation and her words went straight to his cock. He pulled her flush to him and he kenned she could feel his hard length.

Her eyes flared wide and she raised an eyebrow in challenge.

"We arena married yet, Lass."

She shrugged her shoulders. "Doesna matter. We will be."

He glanced over her shoulder at Mary, who, as always, hung back far enough to not interrupt, but still made her presence known.

Saint's above he wanted to take Lizzie up on her offer. He'd been thinking about losing himself in her softness all night. He didn't think his body could hold off much longer.

"What of Mary?"

"She can stay in the room I rented for her and I. And I..." She walked her fingers up his chest and he swore he never felt anything more erotic. "I can go to your room with ye."

Emotions warred within him. He kenned he shouldn't. Not until they were married. He should be a reputable man and hustle her inside her room and retire to his own for the night. But Hell's teeth, he didn't have the willpower to deny her. Not when she looked up at him with those big brown eyes burning bright for him.

But the choice was still hers. He would not force her into doing something she did not want to do. He refused to pressure her. Such an act would not be in his nature.

Nay, he would offer her an exit clause, just in case she was only telling him what she thought he wanted to hear because he was standing right in front of her.

He pushed open the door to her room and tilted his head. "Go on inside, Lass."

Confusion marred her face, and she looked crestfallen. Dejected.

With a finger under her chin, he lifted her face to his. "Dinna fash. Ye control your fate. Speak with Mary. Think on what ye really want. The choice is yours and there is no right or wrong answer. Whate'er ye decide, I will abide by and 'twillna change my feelings. If ye still want to spend the night in my bed, come to room 11. But remember, only if ye are sure. Because I guarantee ye, if ye show up at my door, I dinna think I will e'er be able to let ye go."

He bent and kissed her forehead. "Now go. And if I dinna see ye later, I bid ye good night and will see ye in the morn."

Turning on his heel, he made his way up the stairs to his own room. Sitting on the bed, he cradled his head in his hands and blew out a steadying breath. Not daring to hope that he would get a knock on his door.

His luck had already blessed him ten-fold today with everything that had happened. He'd be a fool to think his streak would continue through the night.

And he wasn't mad about that. Nay. If Lizzie wanted to wait until their wedding night, he had no qualms about that. As he'd told her the choice was hers and he wouldn't push her one way or another.

He was still sitting on the bed, contemplating all the events of the day, when the slightest knock sounded.

His breath caught in his throat.

Was it Lizzie?

Were the saints again blessing him on this day? He stood and pushed his hands through his hair and took a deep breath before letting it out slowly, trying to calm his racing heart.

The knock came again. A little louder this time.

Hurrying to the door, he swung it open, and his heart melted at the sight standing before him.

There Lizzie stood, in her night dress and robe. But the ties of her robe hung at her sides, allowing him to see the outline of curves through the thin material of her night dress.

A moan escaped his lips, and she smiled.

Before he allowed her entry, he needed one more confirmation. Just as much for him as for her.

"Are ye sure, Lass?" he whispered.

She nodded, licking her lips. "I have ne'er been more sure of aught in my life."

That was all he needed to hear.

Grasping her hand, he pulled her inside the room, flush against his chest and kicked the door shut with his boot and crushed his mouth down on hers in a searing kiss that let her ken there was no going back now. Before this night was over she would be claimed as his in the most intimate way possible.

Her hands snaked around his neck, and he was frustrated at the barrier of material stopping him from feeling the crush of her breasts against his chest.

Breaking the kiss, he shrugged out of his jacket, then loosened his cravat and threw it the floor. His shirt followed, and he smiled proudly at her rounded eyes. She reached out tenderly and palmed his chest, running her hands up and down his skin. Over the ridge of muscles of his abdomen.

He sucked in a breath and blew it out in a hiss.

"Ye are wicked, Lass," he taunted.

She looked concerned.

"In the best of ways," he quickly added, cradling her face in his hands, rubbing his thumbs along her cheeks. He dipped his head and captured her mouth once again, dropping his hands to the curve of her buttocks and pulled her closer, reveling in her nearness. The feel of her ample breasts against his chest.

Without breaking the kiss, he walked her back to the bed. Once there, he stepped back, enjoying the sight of her. He caressed her cheek, and she closed her eyes, leaning into his touch. She bit her lip, and it was one of the sexiest things he'd ever witnessed. He hooked the collar of her robe and slid it down her slender arms and marveled at the way her skin pebbled as it was exposed to the air.

And to him.

He bent and grasped the hem of her night dress. Looking into her eyes, he couldn't help but ask one last time. "Ye sure?"

"I have ne'er wanted aught more."

He lifted the gossamer material, slowly exposing the pale skin of her thighs, and then her mound. Her flat stomach, and finally her ample breasts. Her rosy nipples were hard, jutting out to him. Calling to him. He couldn't wait to suck them into his mouth.

Pulling the garment over her head, he let it fall to the floor and he gazed upon the goddess standing before him. She met his eyes, and hers were dark with passion, as she stood proudly, letting him drink in the image of her.

She made no move to hide herself from his gaze, and he found that so enticing.

"Sit on the edge of the bed, Lass," he ordered gently and she complied without question.

He bent, boxing her in with his arms at her sides and captured her mouth once again, as he gently pushed her to lay back. When she had sunk into the mattress, her legs dangling off the side, he moved to his knees. Grasping her right ankle, he kissed the sensitive skin on the inside of her ankle, trailing his lips up the inside of her leg, until he was at the apex of her thighs.

Her scent infiltrated his senses, driving him mad with need. He had to fight the urge to plunge himself into her slick wetness. He could see her arousal dripping from the seam of her nether lips. He draped her leg over his shoulder, and then did the same with her left.

Then he settled in for the best meal of his life. Blowing on the damp curls, he smiled as she wriggled her bottom. When he darted his tongue out and ran it along her wet seam, she gave a squeal of surprise, and her hands fisted the duvet.

She tasted divine. Like heaven itself had been laid out before him to feast upon. He licked up and down her folds and then suckled the bud of nerves and she bucked her hips off the bed.

"Malcolm," she gasped, and he smiled against her.

Sinking a finger into her soft folds, he took his time letting her get adjusted to the sensation, slowly dragging his finger in and out, and when her juices flooded his hand, he added a second finger, and then another.

Lizzie moved her hands to his head, fisting his hair, as she tried to pull him even closer.

He smiled at her passion.

When her hips undulated, matching the rhythm of his strokes, he kenned she was ready for him. He stood, and she cried out.

"Nay!"

He bent and kissed her lips, kenning she could taste herself. "Dinna fash, lass. I need to get out of my breeches."

She sat up to lean on her elbows and licked her lips as she watched him unfasten his breeches and slide them down his legs. Her eyes rounded as his cock jutted straight forward, hard as stone, and her tongue peaked out through her lips.

Kicking off his pants, he dropped on the bed beside her and pulled her close as he settled them in the middle of the bed. He brushed her mussed hair from her flushed cheeks.

She trailed her hand down his chest, down the muscles of his stomach, through the nestle of curls. He snatched her hand to stop her from going any further for fear of spending himself right then and there. He was so close to the edge. It wouldn't take much to send him toppling over. And her hand around his cock would surely drive him mad.

"Ye ready?" he asked.

She nodded, as he moved on top of her and settled between her thighs, his cock resting at her entrance.

"Ye will feel a pinch, but I'll do my best to make it as painless as possible, love."

She nodded, lifting her head to capture his mouth in a kiss.

He took the opportunity of that distraction and plunged inside, breaking her barrier. He felt her cry against his mouth, and he stilled his hips, allowing her to adjust to him. He continued to kiss her, then moved his lips to her neck, and nuzzled her there, then her left breast and took the turgid nipple into his mouth, suckling it until she cried out his name on a sigh, and began to move her hips.

Used to the sensation of him, he pulled his hips back, then pressed forward slowly, and was blessed with the most beautiful moan. He wanted to hear that moan for the rest of his life.

He continued pumping his hips slow, though he wanted naught more than to drive himself to the hilt into her over and over. But that was for another time.

He was so close to spending himself and was thankful when her hips began to move faster. Her hands dropped to his buttocks, pushing him forward.

"What do ye want, Lass?"

Confusion marred her face. "I, I dinna ken. I want...more? I dinna ken. I feel—"

He pushed forward, burying himself deep.

"Ah," she sighed. "More, more of that."

He repeated the move a few times and her moans grew. Her skin heated as she squeezed her eyes shut. "There's something happening. Something building," she whispered, her voice a mix of confusion and awe.

Reaching down between them, he circled her bud of pleasure, adding an amount of pressure to the circles, and that was all it took. Underneath him her body stiffened, around his cock, her sex milked him. He pumped harder, and her fingernails scored his back as she called his name.

Unable to hold back any longer, he thrust deep a final time, and reached his own climax in a sea of stars behind his eyes as he stiffened and emptied his seed into her, his body convulsing with each jet of his release.

Their breaths coming in short gasps, he kissed her lips on a smile and rolled over, dragging her with him.

Tucking her head beneath his chin, he kissed her forehead.

"How do ye feel, Lass?"

"Wonderful," she answered, her voice soft and sleepy.

"Any regrets?"

"Nay." He felt her shake her head against his chest, then placed a kiss over his heart.

"Good. I love ye, Lass," he whispered into her hair.

"I love ye, Malcolm," she whispered back, her palm splayed across his heart and yawned.

"Sleep, love," he ordered gently. "We've a busy day ahead of us tomorrow."

LIZZIE WOKE IN the early hours of the morning, the room was still dark, and Malcolm slept soundly beside her.

At some point he'd settled them under the covers, and she was snuggled with her back spooned to his front.

She felt sore, but in the best of ways. She had heard about sex in snippets she'd caught of conversations, but she never once thought it would be as amazing as what she and Malcolm had shared last night.

Wriggling her butt, she could feel Malcolm's hardness against the back of her thighs.

"Lass," he murmured. "If ye dinna cease your movement, I will have to love ye again," he said sleepily.

"Oh?" She kind of liked that idea, so she wriggled her butt again, pushing it back so there was no way he could not feel her.

With a growl, he pulled her even closer and nipped at her neck.

She squealed in delight and then moaned as he entered her from this angle, thrusting his hips into her from behind.

"Oh," she said again, but this time it was from the sensations this angle was eliciting. It was so different from last night, but just as enticing.

He sucked her lobe into his mouth, and she moaned. Her nerves felt as if they were on fire. With every push of Malcolm's hips, the fire grew. Forming in her belly, and growing, until it became a fireball that she couldn't contain. It consumed her, and when his hand snaked between them, through her nestle of curls to make circular motions on the bundle of nerves at the apex of her thighs, she lost all control of her body.

Her limbs stiffened, her belly contracted, as tremors wracked her body, and colors burst in her eyes.

Behind her, Malcolm quickened his pace, and soon he was crushing her to him, calling out her name in a guttural voice that seemed divinely primal, and shuddered uncontrollably behind her as he thrust as deep as he could.

She grasped his fingers, kissing each one, as they let their shudders subside.

When she could speak, she broke the silence. "I want to wake up like that every morn."

Behind her, Malcolm's chest rumbled with laughter. "If that is what ye wish for, I will be sure to make that happen." He buried his face in her neck, and frissons shot up and down her body.

Laying in the warmth of Malcolm's strong arms, the steady staccato of his heartbeat vibrating against her back, her eyelids soon grew heavy and she drifted off to sleep once again.

When she woke, a tray of tea and scones was set beside her on the bed, and Malcolm was dressed, reading a paper in the chair, his legs crossed.

Hearing her stir, he put down the paper and smiled warmly. "Good morn."

She sat up, stretching her arms, but being careful not to spill the pot of tea beside her. "To ye, as well." She poured a cup of tea, adding a cube of sugar and bit into a buttery scone. "What is the plan for today?"

The seriousness of their activities of the past night flooded her mind.

"We go to Tolton Hall. And I will officially ask for your hand in marriage. Unless of course, ye've changed your mind."

"Absolutely no'!" She said vehemently. "I canna wait to be your wife."

He walked over to her, bent and placed a kiss on her forehead. "And I canna wait to be your husband. Now, eat up. Mary has your bag packed and ready to go and dropped off a gown for ye."

"I am impressed. Ye have thought of e'erything."

"Well, I clearly couldna have ye running around in your night clothes," he chuckled.

Later, when they'd arrived back at Tolton Hall, and Papa gave his overzealous approval of their marriage, Lizzie learned that Mama kenned she had no intention of visiting Rosalyn.

"Please, Lizzie. Ye forget I am your mother. 'Twas no' that long ago that ye told us ye were going to visit a friend, only to be caught by Malcolm. And ye canna tell me there was no spark or feelings there. They were apparent to a blind man."

Papa chuckled. "Your mother has a well-made point."

"Ye had been miserable since Malcolm left. Did ye think I didna realize that ye were spending that whole time plotting how to get to back to him? 'Twas just a matter of time until ye contrived your plan and approached us with it."

Wow, her parents had read her like a book. "That's why ye gave me the phaeton. And the coachman."

"Aye, and when you got down the road, he kenned ye were going to switch destinations. He was there to ensure ye were safe."

Beside her, Malcolm guffawed. "It looks like your parents had your plan figured out as if they'd come up with it themselves."

"Apparently."

"Well," Mama said, clapping her hands, "if ye gentlemen will excuse us. We've a wedding to plan."

Two months later

SURROUNDED BY FAMILY and friends, which included Malcolm's best friends and all their wives, save for Gunn, who somehow, was still single, she and Malcolm pledged their vows to each other.

The party that followed was the talk of the town, and when they left for Culzean Castle, they were given a grand send off.

They waved at everyone as they left. Mary had already made the journey to Culzean. She would stay in her position as Lizzie's maid.

Lizzie snuggled into Malcolm's side. His arm was draped around her, and his lips lingered on her hairline.

"Do ye remember when we were first journeying to Tolton Hall so I could prove my innocence?" she asked.

"Aye."

"And ye told me that ye belonged to no one. That ye were nobody's man?"

"Aye," he said again.

"I guess I proved ye wrong," she said smugly. "Because obviously, ye are my man."

He growled and nipped at her ear.

Then in a flash, he was kneeling in front of her, lifting her skirts.

He waggled his eyebrows. "Have I e'er shown ye how much fun a carriage ride can be?"

"Ye ken ye havena."

"Well, then. Time to rectify that, I'd say."

His head disappeared under her skirts and his mouth found her core.

She threw her head back with a sigh. Enjoying the ride in more ways than one.

EPILOGUE

MALCOLM AND LIZZIE settled onto the sofa in Viscount Wilson's study. The viscountess sat in a chair beside the roaring fire. The weather had grown cold and even with the fire, the air in the room still held a chill that hung heavy in the air.

"When ye called for a visit, Lord Kennedy, I was surprised. I believe we are all settled in our payment for your services."

Malcolm smiled. "Aye. We are fine there. I just thought ye may be interested in learning that I have uncovered the identity of the Phantom Prowler. Well, no' me per se, but my lovely wife."

In the chair, the viscountess visibly paled.

Wilson furrowed his brow. "I dinna recall hearing an announcement."

"Aye. We thought we should discuss it with ye. To allow ye to decide how to deal with it in your way."

"I am confused."

Lizzie had remained silent until this moment. "Viscountess Wilson," she announced. "Is there something ye would like to confess? Or should I?"

"My lady. I—" The viscountess paused, looking nervously at her husband.

"What is it?" he snapped. "I've other business to attend this day."

"Your wife, Viscount," Lizzie said. "The Phantom Prowler has been right under your nose this whole time."

His eyes flew to his wife, who looked at the floor instead of meet-

194

ing his gaze. "Is this true?"

Kenning she had been caught and cornered, she confessed to what she'd done. All the while her husband fumed, his ruddy face even redder than usual.

"I just wanted some excitement. Our everyday lives have become so monotonous."

"Do ye realize how much ye have put us at risk? What is at stake? We could lose everything," the viscount spat, disgust clear on his face.

That was Malcolm's cue to leave. He stood, holding his hand out for Lizzie to take. "We have told no one else due to your status. We will leave it up to ye to decide how to move forward. Though we suggest somehow returning the jewels and items that were stolen to their rightful owners. Have a good afternoon."

Malcolm held his arm out to Lizzie and she slipped her hand into the crook and they walked out together into their waiting carriage.

Settled inside, she gave him a sly look.

He kenned that look. The wicked gleam in her eyes. His body roared to life.

"What are ye thinking, Lass?" He asked.

"'Tis quite the journey back home."

"Aye?"

She trailed her index finger down his chest, then tapped it against his heart. "How to pass the time?" She cocked her head to the side and clucked her tongue. Her fingers pulled on his cravat, and he pulled her onto his lap, burying his face in her bosom.

"Two can play at this game, Lass," he said, pushing the sleeve of her gown off her shoulder, trailing kisses down the column of her neck.

She sighed and pulled him up to capture his lips.

"I love ye so much, Malcolm, my nobody's man."

ABOUT THE AUTHOR

Award-winning author Brenna Ash is addicted to coffee, chocolate, and all things Scotland and BTS. She's a firm believer that one can never have too much purple or glitter. She loves rom-coms and always cries at the HEAs.

When she's not busy writing about sexy, Scottish Highlanders, Medieval Pirates, Regency Rogues, or co-hosting the true crime podcast, Crime Feast, she spends her time reading with her favorite music playing in the background, binge-watching Outlander and Bridgerton, park-hopping with her besties, spoiling her cat, Lilly, or watching BTS content online. Brenna lives with her husband on the Space Coast in sunny Florida.

Website – www.brennaash.com
Amazon – amazon.com/stores/author/B01H46ZA02
Facebook – facebook.com/BrennaAshAuthor
Instagram – instagram.com/brennaashauthor
BookBub – bookbub.com/profile/brenna-ash

Made in the USA
Las Vegas, NV
09 April 2025

20728208R00115